AMONG MORTALS

THE STORY OF THE

A Retelling for Young Readers

Ranjit Rauniyar, Suhani Rauniyar, Ranveer Rauniyar

Illustrated by Swetha Girishkumar

THE THIRSTY SCHOLAR PRESS
LONDON

AMONG MORTALS AND GODS: The Story Of The Ramayana

First Edition: October 2025

ISBN 978-1-918217-10-0 (paperback)
ISBN 978-1-918217-07-0 (harcover)
ISBN 978-1-918217-08-7 (ebook)

Publisher: The Thirsty Scholar Press
London, United Kingdom
Publisher contact: publisher@thethirstyscholarpress.com

Illustrated by: Swetha Girishkumar
Interior design and formatting by: Melvyn Paulino (melvyn@branddor.com)

The Ramayana is an ancient Sanskrit epic traditionally attributed to Sage Valmiki. This work is the authors' interpretation and retelling of the classic text.

Katha Marg | The Story Trail

In Loving Memory

for mummy and daddy

for dadi and dadu

Acknowledgements

THIS BOOK IS A RETELLING OF THE RAMAYANA FOR YOUNG READERS, and also a journey that allowed me to fully draw and immerse my children in the love, learning, and deeper understanding of this sacred text.

To our incredible friends and family: your time and thoughtful feedback through early drafts have been invaluable, as has your encouragement and support.

A heartfelt thank you to:

Bedashree Bhattacharjee, Riya Chandra, Sagar Dewan, Shivani Gautam, Nivi Gideon, Gaurika Gupta, Samyuktha Iyer, Nikhilesh Jha, Binay Kumar Kushiyait, Aneesh Maloo, Advay Mathur, Vaibhav Mehra, Aryan Minocha, Sanjeev Minocha, Aruna Puri, Praneeti Rauniyar, Prianka Rauniyar, Rajesh Rauniyar, Ravi Rauniyar, Namrata Sarma, Iqra Shamim, Harmit Singh, Kriti Tyagi, Nandini Vakil, Natasha Vasdev, Srini Venkata, Keya Vinay, and Natasha Vohra.

Thank you also to our beta readers - Jamie Barry, J. Flowers-Olnowich, and Joshua Powell - for suggesting tweaks and insights that might not have crossed our minds on our own. Your thoughtful questions, such as why Manthara opposed Rama's coronation so fiercely, encouraged us to delve deeper into the underlying layers of this epic, illuminating aspects of the story that we, as 'inheritors,' might have otherwise missed.

Special thank you to Joshua Grubb and Kaitlyn Fitzsimmons - your editorial care, insights, and skilful tightening of the language have brought clarity and strength to these pages. As Western readers approaching this narrative from outside its cultural tradition, you brought something essential - the distance and perhaps even the detachment necessary - to provide a perspective both fresh and unencumbered.

Most of all, I want to thank my lovely wife Surbhy - also darling mum and indulger-in-chief. She is not just the heart of our family but also the soul of this project. Her love, humour, and belief have been the foundation of everything the children do. This book is as much hers as it is ours.

This project is so special to us; knowing it has found its way into your hands and homes gives us untold joy. Thank you for helping us bring this cherished retelling of the *Ramayana* to life - your love and encouragement mean more to us than these words can ever express.

Preface

OUR FIRST INTRODUCTION TO THE ENCHANTING WORLD OF THE *Ramayana* was in Grade 4 at The British School in New Delhi, where we found ourselves dazzled by the *Ramlila*, a dramatic enactment of the story of Rama, the beloved ancient Hindu king. While the finer details of our performance remain blurry, what we carry with us still are the vivid splashes of red and yellow costumes and the immaculate energy, music, and dancing that formed part of this great play.

This story re-entered our lives on our tenth birthday, during which time we chose a six-volume set of Valmiki's *Ramayana* as a return gift for our friends.

A few days later, we attempted to read through a spare copy of this seemingly child-friendly, colourful comic-style book with our parents. Despite its visual appeal, the convoluted details caused our interest to slump long before the demon king Ravana and the crafty Manthara could fully cast their spells and unleash the dark forces.

Yet over the years, our encounter with the heroic antics of our favourite Hanuman *ji*, the touching valiance of the vulture king Jatayu, and the riveting battle scenes between the *vanara* army and the *rakshasas* in Lanka continued to spark our imagination.

The importance of the *Ramayana* is, unfortunately, undermined by its inaccessibility; it has only ever made appearances in overly simple picture books for little children or books for grown-ups that are far too unwieldy and esoteric for a young person to sit down and read, much less enjoy. For this reason, it became incredibly important to us to bring this story directly and simply to young readers as best as we have been able to do here, while remaining true to its complex and nuanced storyline, and ageless ideals.

With its retelling here, we hope to draw you into this ancient narrative - rich not only in wisdom but also in culture and history - so that it rises beyond these pages and fills your heart with messages of strength, honour, and sacrifice, especially in a time when these values sometimes appear frayed.

Together with our dad, we have enjoyed researching, reading, writing, and editing this book for six years now. We feel great joy to know that this treasure of a story has found its way to you, wherever you are in the world, to give you company, bring you comfort, and fill you with delight.

Warmly,
Suhani Rauniyar, Ranveer Rauniyar

Hertfordshire, England
October 2025

The Heroes and Villains of The Ramayana

1. **Of the Gods of the Universe: (Trimurti – Three Divine Forms)**
    - *Brahma (The Creator)*
    - *Vishnu (The Preserver)*
    - *Shiva (The Destroyer)*
2. **Of the Kingdom of Kosala**

    King Dasharatha
    - **His Wives**: *Kaushalya, Sumithra, Kaikeyi*
    - **His Sons**: *Rama (son of Kaushalya), Lakshmana and Shatrughna(twin sons of Sumithra), Bharata (son of Kaikeyi)*
    - **His Daughters-in-law**: *Sita (married to Rama), Urmila (married to Lakshmana)*
    - **His Royal Priest**: *Sage Vasishta*
    - **Handmaiden to Queen Kaikeyi**: *Manthara*
3. **Of the Kingdom of Videha**

    King Janaka
    - **Daughters**: *Sita (adopted), Urmila*
4. **Of the Kingdom of Lanka**

    King Ravana
    - **Uncles**: *Maricha, Subahu*
    - **Sister**: *Shurpanakha*

- **Brothers**: *Vibhishana, Kumbhakarna, Khara, Dushana*
- **Wives**: *Mandodari, others*
- **Sons**: *Meghanada (eldest), later known as Indrajit after he defeated Indra, (King of the Gods); others*

5. **Of the Kingdom of Kishkindha:**

   King Sugriva

   - **Brother**: *Vali*
   - **Nephew**: *Angada (Vali's son)*
   - **Hanuman**

6. **Sage Vishwamitra**

7. **Jatayu (Vulture)**

8. **Sampati (Vulture)**

9. **Garuda (Eagle)**

10. **Jambavana (Bear)**

CHAPTER 1

The Great King Dasharatha and an Heir for Kosala

OUR STORY OF THE RAMAYANA BEGINS IN AYODHYA, AN ANCIENT city founded by the first ruler of the Solar Dynasty, King Manu. Nestled along the banks of the gentle Sarayu River, Ayodhya, meaning 'the invincible city,' thrived as the bustling capital of the kingdom of Kosala.

At the time our story is set, Kosala was ruled by King Dasharatha.

The portraiture we have of Dasharatha is that of a great king - wise, able, and fearless.

While Ayodhya brimmed with splendour, its power and prosperity did not affect its pleasant and welcoming atmosphere - the air carried a soft, sweet fragrance, and the sun splashed its energy and warmth upon the city's streets. With its grand palaces, temples, and forts, the kingdom was unmatched in its architecture and culture. Its people, as warriors, scholars, merchants, artisans, farmers, or labourers, were so devoted to their duties that a more perfect place could not be found on Earth.

In the magnificent city of Ayodhya, every sunrise seems to bless its people,

and every corner whispers tales of its legendary kings.

Indeed, King Dasharatha ruled over the kingdom with wisdom and fairness, leaning on the counsel of his ministers, advisors, and royal priests.

The traditions of *satya* (truth) and *dharma* (duty) were not just enduring virtues but the very essence of life for the king, his family, and his people, guiding their every thought and action.

Everyone in the kingdom was happy and contented.

Everyone, alas, but for King Dasharatha himself.

As the great king grew older, a deep melancholy took hold of him. Though blessed with the love and companionship of his three queens - Kaushalya, Sumithra, and Kaikeyi - King Dasharatha was haunted by the absence of an heir to the throne.

Often, he was seen to be withdrawn, lost in his thoughts, his figure slumped in the oppressive quiet of his longing.

Beneath the Crown lay the unbearable grief of King Dasharatha for an heir to his kingdom.

King Dasharatha confided his deep-seated anguish to Sage Vashishta, his trusted royal priest. "Nothing weighs more heavily on my spirit," the king confessed. "What cruel irony, is it not, to rule this loving, prosperous kingdom yet feel as hollow and pained from within?"

Sage Vashishta listened intently as the king continued. "I have braved many storms, but this unending sea of sorrow terrifies me. I fear its dark, haunting gloom may fall over the kingdom, troubling my queens and my people long after I am gone."

Sage Vashishta placed a comforting hand on the king's shoulder. "Your Majesty, do not lose heart. This burden is not yours alone to carry. Let me turn this over in my heart - there may yet be a path forward."

Days passed as the sage contemplated the king's plight, searching through ancient texts and meditating on possible remedies.

When Vashishta returned to the palace, his eyes held new hope. "Your Majesty, I believe there is a way. We must explore a remedy that could lift this burden." He counselled the king to undertake a yagna (a sacred fire ritual) to seek heavenly favour and be blessed with an heir he so dearly longed for.

Just as these concerns were playing out on Earth, in heaven, the *devas* (gods) were grappling with a grave threat of their own. The ten-headed *rakshasa* (demon) Ravana - whose evil eclipsed all others across the *triloka* (the three worlds: heaven, earth, and the netherworld) - had been inflicting untold suffering on the innocents. As the dark influence of Ravana's reign expanded unchecked, it spared no one.

Desperate and fearful, the gods gathered before Lord Brahma, the Creator of the Universe, and turned to him for help. "Ravana bends to no one's will but his own," they pleaded, "and commands fear unlike any before him. He threatens to plunge all the realms into complete darkness. His power is greater than even our own. What would you have us do?"

But why, you may wonder, couldn't one of the gods simply slay Ravana and rid the realms of his terror? The answer lay in the gods' own divine promise that now protected him. In his youth, Ravana had devoted endless years performing the great *tapasya* (penance), reaching such profound levels of meditation, austerity, and spiritual discipline that it moved the heavens to grant him two mighty blessings: the boon of infinite strength bestowed by Lord Shiva, the Destroyer of the Universe, and from Lord

Brahma, the boon that no god or demon would ever have the power to end his life.

A boon, once granted, could not be taken back.

With boons from Brahma and Shiva, Ravana's tapasya makes him invincible against gods, yet he forgets that there is great folly in hubris.

However, not all hope was lost. Lord Brahma noticed a crucial flaw in the blessings Ravana had sought for himself. While it was true that no god or demon could kill him, Ravana - in his arrogance - had failed to seek protection from humans, whom he deemed too weak to pose any real threat.

At Lord Brahma's urging, the gods assembled before Lord Vishnu, who, as the Preserver of the Universe, offered a solution: "To end Ravana's reign of terror and restore peace, I shall take an avatar (incarnate) in human form."

INCARNATION

Incarnation (*avatar*) in the Hindu religion means 'rebirth.' It is when a divine entity manifests in a physical/human form and descends to the mortal world (Earth), often to counteract the forces of evil and restore cosmic balance and order.

In the story of Ramayana, Rama is an incarnation of Lord Vishnu (the Preserver of the Universe). Lord Krishna, a central figure in the second Hindu epic, *The Mahabharata*, is also an incarnation of Lord Vishnu. According to Hindu scriptures, Lord Vishnu has taken a human or animal form ten times (*dashavatara*) since the inception of the Universe, including incarnations as a tortoise (*Kurma*), fish (*Matsya*) and man-lion (*Narasimha*).

The concept of incarnation is rooted in the idea that it becomes necessary to mend the rifts between good and evil when darkness seeks to overshadow light to disrupt the natural order.

This concept of incarnation is significant in other religions too. In Christianity, for example, consider this passage from the Bible: "For God so loved the world that he gave his one and only son, that whosoever believeth in him shall not perish but have eternal life." (John 3:16).

According to the Christian faith, Jesus Christ was an incarnation of God who came to Earth in human form to redeem humanity from its sins. His crucifixion and resurrection not only symbolise the ultimate sacrifice but also proffer to humanity the promise of salvation and eternal life.

Hinduism, Christianity, and other religions share the idea that divine beings can take on physical form to guide, protect, and uplift humans during times of moral and spiritual crises. In other words, incarnations across religions embody empathy and involvement by the gods in the human condition. This intervention signifies God's love and compassion for humanity, bridging the infinite separation between the divine and the human.

Thus, it was agreed that Lord Vishnu would be born as Rama, the son of King Dasharatha of Kosala.

The gods were heartened by Lord Vishnu's pledge to intercede by reincarnating as Rama. They hoped this divine act would tip the scales against the gathering dark forces and energies that had been unleashed by the demon king.

Meanwhile, back on Earth, King Dasharatha's *yagna* was underway with full earnestness. No cost or effort was spared to make this the most pious and celebrated ritual ever, reflecting the deep hopes of the ageing monarch. The ritual lasted a year, culminating in a miraculous event: from the flames of the sacrificial fire emerged a radiant and commanding figure bearing a golden vase filled with *payasa* (a sweet rice pudding). This heavenly figure then instructed the king to share this *payasa* with his queens.

The yagna's flames reach the heavens with the King's deepest prayers, as he awaits a divine intervention for an heir to his kingdom.

DHARMA

Dharma is a religious, ethical, and moral construct that forms the basis of Hinduism. It is the foundation for guiding one's thoughts and conduct, including duties, conduct, laws, and values. *Adharma*, its antithesis, signifies the absence of *dharma*, embodying falsehood, greed, and a lack of conscience and virtue.

In the Brahmanic Universe, an eternal struggle exists between the forces of *dharma* and *adharma*, with *dharma* acting as the stabilising force that maintains balance. The root 'dhar' in *dharma* means "to hold," "to keep from," or "to maintain." Thus, *dharma* is that which upholds or maintains the moral and cosmic order from forces of evil, lies, and deceit.

Dharma is not limited to human actions; it extends to all beings and elements in the universe. For example, it is the *dharma* of a bee to make honey, a cow to provide milk, the sun to radiate warmth and light, the river to flow, and the moon to illuminate the night sky. Harmony and balance in the moral order of the universe are achieved when everyone or everything faithfully adheres to their respective *dharma*s.

The wheel at the centre of the Indian flag, known as the *Ashoka Chakra*, symbolises the concept of *dharma*, highlighting its significance in the nation's identity and values.

King Dasharatha joyfully complied, distributing the contents of the golden vase as he had been instructed. To his first wife, Kaushalya, he gave half the vase's contents. He divided the remaining portion equally between his other two wives, Kaikeyi and Sumithra. "Much joy may this bring my gentle queens," he said.

The *yagna's* blessings were soon realised. Each of King Dasharatha's three wives was blessed with an offspring - or in Queen Sumithra's case, two - a fulfilment that went beyond the King's deepest prayers. Queen Kaushalya gave birth to the eldest son, Rama; Queen Kaikeyi had Bharata; and Queen Sumithra welcomed twin sons, Lakshmana and Shatrughna.

The Kingdom of Kosala marked this gift of not just one, but four noble princes, heralding a new era of peace and prosperity. As Dasharatha, a proud father and king, beheld his children, his eyes lit up for he saw just how much each of his sons was a perfect reflection of his image - an amalgam of grace and the virtues of their ancestors.

Amid these jubilant celebrations, the true significance of Rama's birth remained veiled in mystery. Lord Vishnu's mortal form as Rama was now manifest, but would await his ultimate destiny against Ravana's dark and infernal forces. But that reckoning lay distant yet. For now, there was endless rejoicing throughout the lands at the greatest gift from the gods themselves. At long last, the kingdom of Kosala was blessed with a future king.

CHAPTER 2

The Fellowship of the Princes

KING DASHARATHA DOTED ON HIS FOUR BOYS AND LOVED THEM TO no end - they were each dearer to him than the light of his own eyes and soul. They grew from little boys into well-brought-up young princes, regal and hardy like lions, with bright eyes, shiny hair, and broad shoulders. Yet their true nobility lay within, for they possessed not only the outer markings of royalty but also the inner graces of warmth and kindness.

The queens, too, poured their affection into their children's upbringing, showering them with love and care.

When the princes were toddlers, tumbling about the palace courtyards and chasing each other through the gardens, Queen Kaikeyi often expressed her mother's worry: "My heart skips a beat every time one of them takes a fall." Queen Sumithra, echoing this sentiment, her face alight, would add, "Little darlings as they are."

The princes' days were rich with fun and laughter, filled with the simple bliss of brotherhood and the innocence of youth. Together, they found perfect happiness in each other's company.

King Dasharatha, ever mindful of their destiny as future kings, insisted that his sons learn and master every skill proper and necessary for a prince and future ruler. Under the training of Sage Vashishta, they mastered their physical prowess - becoming strong, athletic, and skilled in archery and the arts of war. They also developed their intellectual minds through the study of literature and the sacred verses of the *Vedas*, the core Hindu spiritual wisdom and teachings. Every part of their education was imbued with the most essential virtue of all - the virtue of character - as embodied in the principles of *satya* and *dharma*.

Under Sage Vashishta's watchful eye, the young princes train to grow up into warriors and scholars

"Boys after my own heart," King Dasharatha was heard to say often, nearly moved to tears with pride at their exquisite skills, deep knowledge, and kind nature.

Though the four brothers got along fabulously well, it became evident that a special bond flourished between Rama and Lakshmana.

While each prince was brave and capable, Rama stood out inimitably by these qualities. Of the brothers, he was the most devoted to his father. King Dasharatha, too, while he treasured all his sons, felt the deepest connection with his eldest.

And so, by their conduct, the princes, especially Rama, had risen in the hearts of the people of Kosala, who loved and revered them. The brothers returned this affection not with mere gestures, but through quiet acts of service: offering alms to the poor, assisting the elderly, seeking the wisdom of sages with humility, and extending kindness to all, regardless of their station. Their dignity did not distance them; it brought them closer to the people, deepening the bond between ruler and realm.

CHAPTER 3

Sage Vishwamitra Arrives in Ayodhya with a Startling Request

ONE DAY, WHEN THE PRINCES WERE STILL YOUNG, AN UNEXPECTED visitor arrived at the gates of the palace.

This visitor was the famed Sage Vishwamitra. King Dasharatha and his family showed great respect to him, bowing down to touch his feet and seeking his blessings. Vishwamitra was a mighty king once, but he left the throne to become a *rishi* (holy man) to follow the paths of the gods. Across the world, everybody uttered Vishwamitra's name with both awe and caution.

He commanded every weapon known to gods and sages, including the most fearsome of them all, the *Brahmāstra*, a weapon so devastating it had the potential to reduce whole worlds to ash. But even more remarkable was his vision: he was able to see events of the past, present and future throughout the *Triloka* - the three realms of existence.

But for all his wisdom and spiritual heft, Vishwamitra had a notorious temper and burning spiritual ambition. One legend told of a time when his anger made him attempt to create a rival universe. This audacious act, which brought the world to the brink, prompted the gods to intervene just in time to prevent disruption to the order of the cosmos.

Such was the force of legend that surrounded him - and yet, in this moment, he came not as a threat, but as an honoured guest.

"Welcome, O sage of great wisdom and strength," King Dasharatha said, greeting him with open arms. "You honour our kingdom with your presence."

Vishwamitra, cutting through formalities, got straight to the point. "I have come to ask a favour."

King Dasharatha felt a surge of curiosity when Sage Vishwamitra revealed his request could only be fulfilled by the king.

"It would be my great honour," King Dasharatha replied, readily excited and curious. "You have only to ask."

Relief softened the sage's stern face at the king's assurance.

"I seek your eldest son, Rama, to accompany me to the forest."

A hush fell over the court. The king's face turned to stone.

Vishwamitra explained that the sacred forests had become battlefields because Ravana's demons and the dark forces commanded by his uncles, Maricha and Subahu, had taken control there. The *rishis* faced harassment as their rituals were disrupted and their holy places defiled by enemy forces.

"The forest night is heavy with dread," the sage added, "and the very order of dharma is under threat. With Rama's help, we can purge the forests of this menace and ensure that sacred rituals can proceed without interruption."

King Dasharatha hesitated, his voice catching in his throat. "O wise Vishwamitra," he began, choosing his words carefully, "your visit brings us compliments, but Rama is still young. How can he, at this tender age, face the iron grip of terror that haunts the ancient forests?"

While the king deeply respected Vishwamitra's divine wisdom and spiritual power, a father's protective instincts stirred within him. The very legends that made the sage so revered - his volcanic temper, his ability to shake the cosmos with his rage - now filled Dasharatha with dread. How could he send his precious son on such a dangerous mission under the care of one whose fury, however righteous, could reshape worlds? The king's heart wrestled between honouring the great sage and shielding his beloved Rama from harm.

And yet, at the back of his mind he knew Vishwamitra never made requests without serious intent - the solemnity of the sage's purpose here too, therefore, could not be denied. The king was conscious that sustaining cosmic equilibrium was a duty that often demanded significant personal sacrifices. Pondering his options, King Dasharatha offered another solution: he would lead his army personally to defeat the *rakshasas*.

"You honour me by deeming my child Rama worthy of accompanying you - yet I would think my army more than capable of dealing with these lowly rakshasas."

The all-knowing and all-seeing Sage Vishwamitra was taken aback by the king's naiveté. No army, however large and mighty, could stand against Ravana's demons. Only Rama possessed this transcendent capability, for the sage knew he was Lord Vishnu's *avatar*.

"Do not be afraid, O King!" Sage Vishwamitra said. "It is by divine will that your son has been chosen for a mission of such great consequence. This is not only the highest acclamation from the gods but also his dharma. I would do as much for you and willingly offer my sons if they were even half as capable."

Notwithstanding Vishwamitra's assurances, King Dasharatha still remained uneasy and asked if the task could wait until Rama was older.

Sage Vishwamitra's patience, however, was wearing thin. "If Rama isn't sent now, he shouldn't be sent at all," he replied sternly. "I am afraid I cannot afford to waste any more time. I have only ten days left to see through the rituals. If you have spoken, and that is your final decision, I shall leave."

A tense silence fell over the courtroom yet again. Dasharatha wrestled with his paternal affection and his kingly duty. Sage Vashishta, who had been listening quietly, approached him. "Rest easy, my king," he said gently. "Your fears are not unfounded, but know that this is no ordinary mission - it carries a divine purpose. Under Sage Vishwamitra's watchful care, Rama will remain safe. Rama's path was set long before our time, though its meaning is only now revealing itself."

King Dasharatha's brow remained furrowed with worry, but Sage Vashishta continued.

"Rama is no ordinary child. He bears the weight of a fate far greater than we can comprehend. If you still hesitate, let Lakshmana go with him. That way they will be together, and under Vishwamitra's keeping, they will master celestial weapons, and their deeds will bring them the favour of the gods."

"That is so. I must keep my promise," King Dasharatha muttered, acknowledging the wisdom in Sage Vashishta's counsel while remaining wary of agitating Sage Vishwamitra any further. "I do not wish to obstruct the path of destiny."

King Dasharatha finally addressed Vishwamitra, gesturing toward his boys. "As it pleases you, venerable sage, here are my sons. I place my faith in your wisdom and their destiny. If they are meant to defend dharma and learn under your guidance, I will not stand in their way." Though his voice still shook, he continued. "They shall remain in your care for as long as you need them. I shall not ask for their return until they have achieved absolute victory and earned your full blessings."

Sage Vishwamitra gave a slight nod. "Set your mind at ease, king. I shall watch over them as my own flesh and blood."

King Dasharatha drew his sons close one final time before releasing them to their destiny. "Go forth with my blessings, my beloved children, and journey well," he said, bidding a heartfelt farewell. "Open your hearts to all that you will learn from the great sage, and hurry home to share those gifts with us."

CHAPTER 4

Into the Forest of Demons: Brothers vs. Beasts

RAMA AND LAKSHMANA LEFT THE PALACE ALONGSIDE SAGE Vishwamitra, venturing into the forest depths. During rest stops along their journey, the sage taught the young princes how to command mystical weapons.

"These aren't ordinary arms but are infused with sacred powers," he explained as he handed them each a weapon. "Sanctified by the gods themselves, they serve more than the cause of battle; they are instruments of dharma." He paused before whispering the secret *mantras* necessary to wield them effectively. "Know that the mightiest bows sing songs of justice, but only in the hands of the righteous," he added. "The strength of these weapons, my children, lies, therefore, not only in their physical form but in the purity and focus of your intentions. True power is found in restraint and the wisdom to use our abilities justly. Always remember that, for this is the most sacred lesson I can impart to you."

Eventually, they arrived at the cursed forest of Dandaka. Once a happy, splendid place, it was now so ghostly from the torments of demons as to find itself without the gentle murmurs of winds, the singing of birds, the chirping of insects, or the spilling of berries and fruits.

Within this forsaken forest lived the monstrous *rakshasi* (demoness) Tataka and her son, Maricha. Each possessed the strength of a thousand elephants and showed nothing but contempt for all living beings. Tataka, leading a band of demons, was always on the hunt - prowling the forests and surviving on the flesh and blood of humans and animals alike.

Despite their youth, Rama and Lakshmana were unafraid. The princes set themselves deeper down the strangled paths of the dead forest. Treading lightly, they surveyed the area around them, alert for any hint of the dreaded Tataka. Chilling cries could be heard throughout, but that would not deter the princes, not in the slightest.

Rama was eager to destroy the demoness's long reign of terror. He skilfully plucked the string of his bow, producing a sharp, piercing sound to draw her attention. His voice rang out, "Show your face, rakshasi! Your days of cruelty are over." His words travelled through the forest, and before long, the ghastly Tataka emerged, charging toward them with such ferocity that whole trees were uprooted in her wake.

As she closed in on the princes, each stomp of her feet caused the ground to tremble. Around her neck, she wore a necklace crafted from human skulls while saliva dripped down from her savage jaws. Her face was grotesquely coarse yet burnt like embers. Her hands ended in claws as sharp as the sharpest daggers, and her bulging eyes appeared to leap out from her skull.

The evil creature looked at them disdainfully. "You haven't got any weapons powerful enough for me and certainly no strength in your childlike, princely bodies." She hissed menacingly as she ripped branches between her monstrous teeth, spitting them in their direction. Before long, she lunged at the princes, threatening to swallow them whole.

The young princes battle their first demon, the fearsome Tataka of the Dandaka forest.

Though they had no battle experience, Rama and Lakshmana stood without fear before Tataka. Behind them, Vishwamitra's voice was calm but urgent. "My dear Rama," he said, "in the face of evil, the pure of heart must stand tallest, unbowed by fear. Focus your mind, invoke the mantras, and let your actions in this moment flow from your inner dharma."

Taking a deep breath, Rama steadied himself, the solemnity of the task entrusted to him reflected in his gaze upon the demoness. Drawing his sword, Rama cut off both of Tataka's arms. Lakshmana struck too, maiming her ears and nose. Yet, despite these wounds, there appeared to be no let-up in Tataka's ferocity.

Sage Vishwamitra had stressed the urgency of defeating her before sunset, since demons gained strength as night fell. "Make haste, young princes," he urged. "The night is vast and completely in thrall to the rakshasas - and it swiftly approaches."

Tataka made herself invisible, but Rama could discern her presence from the sounds of the rocks and weapons she hurled at them, betraying her position. Realising they had no more time to spare, Rama readied his bow and declared, "This will be your end." With that, he released a celestial arrow blessed with divine energy. The weapon flew straight and true, piercing her chest. At last, Tataka fell to the ground, lifeless.

From the heavens, a voice congratulated the young princes for vanquishing the feared demon. The forest, which for so long had been dark, barren, and voiceless, was immediately restored to its former glory. The wind returned, rustling through the trees. Birds took to the skies once more, while animals emerged gingerly from their hiding places, as if waking from a long, draconian spell.

Sage Vishwamitra felt proud as he prepared to reward their bravery and victory. He bestowed upon the princes an assortment of powerful supernatural weapons and also taught them the secret meditative disciplines to call them. "These divine gifts are extensions of your will and the virtues you embody," he reminded them. "Wield them justly, and they shall never fail you."

After defeating Tataka, Rama and Lakshmana accompanied Vishwamitra to his *ashram* (home).

There, they joined him in performing a *yagna*. These solemn rituals demanded flawless recitation of holy texts and *mantras* offered in honour of the gods. The consecrated fire blazed without ceasing for six days and nights as the sages and princes chanted these ancient hymns.

Trouble, however, resurfaced once more as the dawn broke on the sixth day. Ravana's uncles, Maricha and Subahu, and their demon followers descended upon the *ashram*, driven by a thirst for retribution for Tataka's death. They stormed the sacred grounds, kicking up clouds of dust and jabbing at the holy fire with tainted hands. Rama, standing guard over the ritual, felt his anger rise.

He drew one of the divine weapons bestowed upon him by Sage Vishwamitra and struck Maricha's chest with such force that it hurled him hundreds of kilometres away, plunging him into the sea.

Unlike Tataka, whom Rama had considered irredeemable, he saw in Maricha the chance for atonement. Rama's intention, as he let it be known, was not to kill Maricha but to cleanse him in the purifying waters of the sea through mercy and forgiveness.

Having thus dealt with Maricha, Rama and Lakshmana turned their attention to Subahu and the remaining demons, whose actions over the years had left no room for such mercy - their atrocities had crossed the limits of forgiveness. The brothers struck them down one by one. Once the threat was vanquished, the *yagna* continued undisturbed, its final prayers offered in peace.

Sage Vishwamitra rejoiced as these glorious events unfolded, heralding the first signs of a return to cosmic order.

"It's an impossible task for even the finest warriors to face these demons, but your victory at such a tender age speaks to your courage and noble lineage."

The princes bowed before the great sage, gratefully receiving his blessings.

CHAPTER 5

The Breaking of the Shiv Dhanush and Rama's Marriage to the Most Beautiful Princess

HAVING WATCHED HIS YOUNG CHARGES TRIUMPH OVER EVERY TRIAL they faced, Sage Vishwamitra next led them to the glorious city of Mithila, ruled by the wise and noble King Janaka. Its capital, Janakpur - now part of modern-day Nepal - gleamed with beauty and pulsed with the energy of art and learning, its streets alive with music, verse, and the voices of learned men.

Rama and Lakshmana, having got on bravely and gained the admiration of the great sage, were in the best of spirits and confidence.

Indeed, a great destiny awaited Rama, but their journey had a more immediate purpose: to pay respects to the sage's old friend, King Janaka, who had invited him to a grand prayer ceremony.

Janaka, the wise and revered ruler of Mithila, shared a deep and enduring friendship with King Dasharatha, one that had spanned decades.

The kingdom of Mithila, a jewel within the greater dominion of Videha, stood equal in splendour and prosperity to the magnificent Ayodhya. Its wide avenues, lined with golden spires and bustling with life, commerce, and devotion, reflected the wisdom and wealth of its people.

Upon entering Mithila, Rama's attention was irresistibly drawn to the sight of a beautiful young woman standing on her balcony. Her gentle, incomparable beauty arrested his senses. Her hair, which flowed like the finest silk, and her eyes, which shone like the most precious jewels, seemed to cast a spell on her surroundings. Birds fluttered around her as if in joyful celebration, and blossoms fell from the branches of the trees to rest at her feet. The young woman, catching Rama's admiring gaze, held it in return. In that moment, as the warm sunlight fell on them, they were instantly struck by love.

Rama was convinced that she was no mortal but a heavenly being. Eager to discover more, he enquired about her identity. He was told that once, when King Janaka was ploughing his land, he found a radiant baby nestled within the furrows of the field. Without children of his own, he had adopted her and named her Sita. She was thus regarded as the daughter of the Earth and believed to be an incarnation of the Goddess Lakshmi, the deity of Wealth and Fortune.

As the plough struck the soil, a miracle unfolded, and a beautiful infant, born of the earth, was revealed.

Sage Vishwamitra, Rama, and Lakshmana arrived at the palace of King Janaka, where they received a warm welcome. King Janaka held Sage Vishwamitra in high regard and was eager to meet the young princes accompanying him.

King Janaka explained that, given Sita's extraordinary beauty, virtues, and pure origins as the daughter of Mother Earth, he had set a challenge worthy of her. Any man seeking her hand must prove himself not only in physical strength, but also in character, spiritual purity and divine favour - by lifting and stringing the *Shiv Dhanush*, the great bow of Lord Shiva.

Over the years, this daunting trial had drawn the most intrepid warriors from across the land, and from kingdoms near and far. These gallant warriors, each and every one of them, were hoping to prove themselves - but despite their fame and valour, none had managed to shift the *Shiv Dhanush*, much less lift and string it. Doubt began to spread through the kingdom - perhaps no mortal was worthy of Sita? Would King Janaka ever find a match for his beloved daughter?

Sage Vishwamitra quietly smiled as he listened to the familiar legend of the *Shiv Dhanush*. "I should reassure my old friend Janaka, that his quest for a worthy suitor for his daughter has reached its destined end," he thought, glancing at Rama with a knowing smile.

"If someone is triumphant today, I shall be ever joyful," sighed King Janaka, his voice edged with both hope and resignation. His eyes rested on the *Shiv Dhanush*, lying imposingly at the centre of the hall. The massive bow, warmly gleaming under the high lamps, radiated its own aura - at once welcoming and defiant - beckoning the suitors forward even as it warned them away.

By the time Rama and Lakshmana entered the stately palace hall, spectators had already begun to swell. The tension was so palpable it could be cut with a knife; earlier that day, warrior after warrior, prince after prince, had approached the bow with confidence, only to leave in defeat, their heads lowered in dismay.

The audience's attention turned to the young princes from Ayodhya, and whispers rippled through the crowd. "They're so young," someone murmured. "I can't see how they even stand a chance," another remarked.

Sage Vishwamitra, observing the scene, turned to Rama and gestured toward the bow. "Rama, this is your moment. I am eager to see you attempt this. Your success would bring glory to this occasion."

With Sage Vishwamitra's blessing, Rama made his way to the centre of the grand chamber, where dignitaries and representatives from far-flung kingdoms had gathered and waited expectantly.

As Rama approached the bow, he too paused to admire its sheer majesty. The *Shiv Dhanush* rested inside a large iron chest perched atop an exquisitely crafted eight-wheeled chariot. It had taken over five thousand of the kingdom's strongest men to bring the bow to the chambers. He absorbed its legend before finally reaching for it.

To the astonishment of those gathered, the bow, which had defied the strength of countless warriors over these years, yielded effortlessly to Rama's touch and manoeuvre. With steady hands and graceful poise, he not only lifted the bow but also bent and strung it. As he pulled it back to its full draw, the great bow snapped in two.

The bow that none could even lift snaps effortlessly in Rama's hands.

The sound of Rama's feat reverberated through the royal chambers, reaching far beyond its walls to distant kingdoms. A stunned silence bound the hall as if in a spell. It was broken by King Janaka, who sprang to his feet. "Praise be to God!" he exclaimed. "In Rama, the Prince of Ayodhya, we have at last found one worthy of my daughter." What had begun as murmurs of disbelief among the attendees burst into cheers.

The legend of the *Shiv Dhanush* was fulfilled at last.

Meanwhile, in her private chambers, Sita received the news of the feat from one of her handmaidens. Her heart quickened with a joy that she had never felt before. The princely figure who had captured her gaze earlier that day - the one whose presence had stirred something deep within her - was now destined to be her husband.

When King Dasharatha heard of Rama's triumph, he was visibly elated. He had no doubts about the union - Sita's beauty, grace, and virtue were well-known all over the land. The match seemed not merely arranged in Ayodhya but written in the stars. With a full heart, he gave his blessing and made ready for the journey to Mithila. The celebration grew even more joyful as Lakshmana was wed to Urmila, Sita's beautiful younger sister.

Both kingdoms rejoiced. Feasts stretched lavishly for days. The streets of Mithila shimmered with golden lamps - even the heavens joined in, showering their blessings with flowers upon the newlyweds as people danced and sang merrily to music.

CHAPTER 6

Face-off with the Mighty Parashurama - The Sworn Enemy and Avenger of the Kshatriyas

WHEN THE WEDDING FESTIVITIES CONCLUDED, SAGE VISHWAMITRA returned to the mountains to resume his meditation. Meanwhile, King Dasharatha, Sage Vashishta, and the newlyweds set off for Ayodhya, carrying with them the joys of a blessed union. But their journey home darkened with unexpected peril.

Without warning, a violent storm began to gather. The trees shook as merciless winds ripped through the grounds. Dust and debris swirled to form a blinding storm that blotted out the sun. Horses reared, men shielded their faces, and fear crept into the hearts of even the bravest soldiers.

In this turmoil, Sage Vashishta, wise and attuned to forces beyond the natural, discerned the true origin of the storm - it was no everyday phenomenon but the manifestation of Parashurama's wrath.

Parashurama loomed as a figure of terrifying legend, both dreaded and honoured across the land. He carried an old hatred for the *kshatriya* caste - the warrior class to which Rama belonged. His hatred was not born of mere rivalry, but was rooted in deep personal tragedy.

Years earlier, a *kshatriya* king had slain his father. The loss had consumed him entirely, igniting within him a fire of vengeance that had burnt without rest. He had vowed to himself that he would wipe out all the *kshatriyas* from existence.

As the storm raged on, Parashurama emerged into the open with his battle-axe, which appeared to be shining brightly as if on fire. Despite this threat, Sage Vashishta, King Dasharatha, and the others offered him the deference his legend commanded. They approached Parashurama, giving the customary offering of water as a gesture of peace and welcome. This simple act was a plea for calm and an attempt to avoid a deadly confrontation.

The murder of his father by a kshatriya became the sorrow and rage that consumed Parashurama's soul.

Parashurama's long-standing hostility towards the *kshatriyas* was well known, but his current ire stemmed from Rama's deeds in Mithila. He viewed the breaking of the *Shiv Dhanush* as a grave offence - not only to Lord Shiva, whose divine bow it was, but also to himself, a devoted follower of the great deity. The bow's thunderous crack had reached his ears, disrupting his deep meditative state in the Mahendra mountains, pulling him swiftly to confront the prince of Ayodhya.

Responding to what he perceived to be a provocation, Parashurama issued a direct challenge to Rama. "Here, take my bow," he said. "This mighty weapon was given to me by Lord Vishnu himself. If you can string it, I will deem you a worthy adversary."

King Dasharatha, feeling the rising tension, approached carefully with yet another plea for peace. "O, Great Parashurama, I ask you not to instigate a fight with young Rama, especially knowing this to be a time of celebration."

Parashurama brushed past the king's overture with a nonchalant wave of his hand. "Your words hold no sway over me Dasharatha," he declared, his tone cold and dismissive. Rama, who had kept his peace until now, felt anger flare within him at this open disrespect shown to his father.

The young prince addressed Parashurama firmly but respectfully. "O, son of Jamadagni and Renuka, I have listened patiently to your grievances and understand the deep sorrow that fuels your quest for revenge. But I will not allow you to dishonour my father."

Instantly, Rama lifted and strung the bow with ease, then turned to Parashurama and spoke with a quiet authority that held the weight of something much greater than anger. "Shall I invoke this power to undo all that you have gained through these years of tapasya?" The question, simple yet powerful, revealed Rama's divine nature and prompted Parashurama to examine his own arrogance. Parashurama, who had triumphed over kings and humbled empires, now faced a force beyond anything he'd ever known. What struck deepest wasn't Rama's undeniable strength, but his restraint - the divine choice to show mercy when he held absolute power. Parashurama lowered his gaze. "I have misjudged you," he admitted to Rama.

With that understanding, Parashurama accepted the truth - his time had passed. The fires of his vengeance had burnt for long enough.

He bowed before Rama and Dasharatha. Then, without another word, he turned away, withdrawing into the mountains to live out the rest of his days in quiet meditation.

The standoff ended - not in battle, but in understanding, bringing relief to everyone present.

With Parashurama's departure, King Dasharatha and his family resumed their journey back to Ayodhya - to a city that, in the midst of celebrations for the newlyweds, looked no less than heaven itself.

CHAPTER 7

The Calm Before the Storm

OVER THE NEXT TWELVE YEARS, RAMA AND SITA LIVED HAPPILY IN their palace in Ayodhya. Indeed, happier days had never passed in their lives or in the lives of those around them, for their world was filled with song and joy. Scarcely ever parted, they became each other's shadows and sunspots, feeling fully loved and understood in each other's company. Their relationship blossomed with every season. The sun and moon shone brightly upon them, and the winds always brought good omens of everlasting love and togetherness. Their sacred union was marked by deep love and respect, and Rama's devotion to Sita's happiness reflected perfectly the depth of her devotion to him.

CHAPTER 8

The Palace Intrigues

IN THE YEARS THAT FOLLOWED RAMA'S WEDDING, HIS BOND WITH HIS father grew even stronger. Tales of Rama's wisdom, kindness, and courage put joy in the old king's heart. Reflecting on his life's blessings, King Dasharatha felt proud, especially in his quiet moments, that his noble firstborn was proving himself more than worthy to carry forth the royal legacy as king after he was gone.

"As my life has been full of blessings, my heart is at peace," King Dasharatha would reflect as time rendered him more contemplative and frail. "I desire to retreat into the serenity of the forest, in the manner of my ancestors, comforted that my Rama is ready and able to ascend the throne."

In counsel with his ministers, King Dasharatha found his sentiments echoed back. The king was deeply moved by the love and warm affirmation his ministers held for Rama.

He announced his decision to crown Rama the next king of Kosala, with Sita as his queen. Rama and Sita graciously accepted their father's decision, turning their thoughts to the gods and seeking their blessings.

However, destiny had other designs. Scarcely had Rama retired to his chambers when an urgent message summoned him back. King Dasharatha, beset with sudden agitation, declared, "Let this blessed day not wait any longer. We will have the coronation tomorrow itself." A prescient disquiet appeared to be driving the king - a feeling that any delay might invite misfortune.

Thus, the coronation ceremony was scheduled for the very next day, sending the kingdom into a frenzy of preparations and excitement. The announcement spread like wildfire - the kingdom was transformed overnight into a spectacle of merriment and jubilation. Every street and corner bustled with life. Servants rushed about to decorate the entire kingdom. Homes were decked in festive flair as grown-ups and children alike carefully selected their finest attire for this auspicious occasion.

A tide of celebrations sweeps through the kingdom as it prepares for Rama's coronation.

Now, while the whole kingdom rejoiced at the prospect of their beloved Prince Rama's coronation, one person remained starkly at odds with the jubilant mood: Manthara, the hunchbacked handmaiden of Queen Kaikeyi.

Manthara harboured a strong desire for Bharata, Queen Kaikeyi's son, to be crowned king instead of Rama, believing it would secure Kaikeyi's prominence which in turn would protect her own position and sway in the court.

Rushing into Kaikeyi's chambers, Manthara took her place at the queen's feet and broke the news of Rama's upcoming coronation.

Queen Kaikeyi was overjoyed and, in keeping with the royal tradition of rewarding those who bring good news, offered Manthara her gold necklace. However, Manthara refused the gift with obvious contempt.

"Not so fast, you miserable soul," she snapped. Her years of service in the palace had emboldened her to speak with shocking audacity even to the queen herself.

"As Dasharatha's favourite wife, you take satisfaction in all your hold and influence over the king. Now, with Rama becoming king, all this power and favour you enjoy will shift to him and his mother, Kaushalya. Your fortune, meanwhile, will be laid bare."

Queen Kaikeyi, taking Manthara's words in good humour, responded, "Is that truly so terrible?"

Manthara's face stiffened at the queen's seeming unconcern. Knowing the stakes were too high, she sharpened her tone. "I'm not merely another servant, my queen. My loyalty, as steadfast as any you will find, binds me to your cause. I'd be nothing but a fool - a glorious old fool at that - if I kept these misgivings to myself. Tell me, Queen Kaikeyi, do you truly desire to live the rest of your life as their slave?" Her lips curled into a sneer, and her breathing quickened.

Queen Kaikeyi, who was genuinely pleased about Rama's coronation, dismissed Manthara's qualms, attributing them to her wily nature and wild imaginings. She cherished Rama like her own son and believed wholly in his worthiness to be king.

"Rein in your wicked thoughts, Manthara," the queen scolded, "and do not let your venomous words taint your own fortunes. You speak beyond your place, especially about my Rama, who is as dear to me as Bharata, my own son. How can I feel anything but complete happiness at the news of his coronation? Is there anyone on God's earth who is more deserving?"

Manthara was far from impressed. Narrowing her eyes in disbelief, she snarled, "My queen, you seem determined to bear the crown for Rama when it rightfully belongs to Bharata."

Queen Kaikeyi locked eyes with Manthara, her expression stern. "Open not your mouth against Rama. I will hear no more of this."

The serpent's tongue of Manthara would lead Kaikeyi down a path of ultimate betrayal.

But that was not to be. Manthara moved even closer, her voice now dropping to a defiant whisper. "You, my queen, are decidedly naïve, so blind to the cruel fate that awaits you if you do not act, and swiftly at that. Think about it again: is it not peculiar that Rama should appear to you as king as he would to his own mother, while your own flesh and blood, Bharata, is in your own eyes, reduced to a mere slave?"

Her tone turned trenchant. "The day will soon come when you and your son will mean nothing to Rama - no more than an afterthought."

She paused, letting her words work through like poison before her voice dropped to an even darker register. "Mark my words, my queen. Rama will go to the extreme of killing Bharata to secure his iron grip on the throne."

The repeated mention of Bharata's name left Queen Kaikeyi anxious and unsettled, as if her handmaiden had touched her soul - to that most secret part of it - where only a mother can truly feel and know the depths of the love she feels for her child.

With satisfaction, Manthara watched the conflict play across Kaikeyi's face. She seemed pleased with the seed of villainy she knew she had now firmly planted.

Manthara continued, "If not for yourself, think of your son, who has his whole life ahead of him - to either rule as a king or suffer in the shadows as a pauper. Make your decision promptly, my queen, for time is not on your side. Rama and his mother are quick of ear - the calamity that will befall Bharata, O the calamity!"

Doubt began to take root in Queen Kaikeyi's heart. Could it be that the handmaiden's relentless assertions echoed the hidden fears Queen Kaikeyi had long suppressed but never dared to voice?

Driven by a mother's instinct to protect her child, Queen Kaikeyi became terrified at the thought that her son could be condemned to a life of servitude - or even, God forbid, be mercilessly killed.

CHAPTER 9

The Burden of a Promise and the Banishment of a Prince

KING DASHARATHA, WHO HAD COME PERSONALLY TO INFORM QUEEN Kaikeyi of Rama's coronation, was distressed at the sight of her weeping in the *Kop-Bhawan*, the chamber kept for mourning.

He approached her with concern, "What grieves my queen when my whole kingdom rejoices?"

The Queen took a moment before answering.

"Go on, my queen, you cause me worry," the King said gently.

"Very well then," Queen Kaikeyi said with a noticeable sigh. "There is something urgent that I must ask of you, my king, and I will bring myself to speak only if you promise to grant it."

King Dasharatha, ever trusting in his favourite wife's good nature, readily assured her. "Without question, my dear. Whatever it is you wish, so it shall be."

But Queen Kaikeyi did not want to leave anything to chance. She made King Dasharatha swear an oath, ensuring that there would be no room for doubt or retractions. "Swear to me on Rama," she demanded, "swear you will not break your word." Her gaze, piercing and intent, searched his eyes for any hint of doubt. Only when fully satisfied did she proceed.

"My dear king," Queen Kaikeyi said, her voice trembling. "I have been nothing but a loving and devoted wife, dedicating my heart and soul to your happiness and well-being.

"Do you recall that day when we faced the asuras in battle?"

"Yes, of course, I do," said King Dasharatha. "How could I forget?"

"You should also remember that I saved your life then?" Queen Kaikeyi reminded him.

During that battle, Queen Kaikeyi, in a brilliant act of courage, steered the king's chariot to safety while he lay wounded and unconscious. She had then nursed him back to full health, carefully removing the arrows that remained lodged in his body. A grateful Dasharatha then granted her two wishes but would never have imagined that they would be claimed years later as weapons against his own heart.

Queen Kaikeyi made it clear that her son, Bharata, should be crowned king in place of Rama. That was not all - she called for Rama to be sent to the forest for fourteen years. "Return these promises that are owed to me," she said firmly. "Grant me this so I may continue to regard you as a king of honour, true to your noble bloodline."

King Dasharatha could hardly believe his ears. Pain shot through his body like wildfire; his face turned pale and deathly as he slumped to his knees.

The choice before him was cruel - between his dear, beloved son and a sacred promise made to his devoted wife long ago.

None of this made any sense to him - it broke against everything he believed true. Could it be that he was trapped in a terrible dream or that an evil force was weaving an illusion? But why? To what purpose? How could Queen Kaikeyi, whom he loved wholly and endlessly, bring herself to wound him so deeply?

Perhaps this was a trial set forth by the gods, the king thought. "But surely not - what would they gain from my suffering?" he wondered.

Turning his attention back to his queen, he shot back. "What has come over you? A mother's heart should seek to protect her child, but this? Don't your words burn on your tongue? Don't you feel the tremor in your soul? Rama has always treated you with no less affection than he has his own mother, and he looks to Bharata no less lovingly as his own brother."

But Queen Kaikeyi would hear nothing of it. She felt a strange force working inside her. "Your love for Rama blinds you, my lord," she declared. She brushed aside King Dasharatha's offers of other riches. She appeared driven by a hypnotic fealty to her son that now obscured the love and warmth that had once filled her heart.

Breathing heavily with distress, the king replied, "My Rama, against whom you have plotted so much hate, is the Rama without whom I cannot live. He is most deserving to be king - Rama, loved by you and his people! Is he the same Rama you have hardened your heart against and wish to banish, to a forest no less, to live among demons and beasts for fourteen long years? And what of our lovely Sita - our dear innocent child? What will become of her? Have you thought of that? How can this be right? You might as well have plunged a dagger into my soul. Even the gods will not be able to forgive you for this!"

Queen Kaikeyi remained unmoved, her face a wall of defiance that no plea or persuasion could break.

King Dasharatha adopted a softer, more conciliatory tone in a last-ditch effort to sway her. "Take the kingdom, my dear queen, and bestow it upon Rama with your own hands. It is yours to give him, and your name shall forever shine."

But Queen Kaikeyi's expression remained as stoic as a cliff, unmoved by the batterings of these stormy seas.

King Dasharatha resorted to invoking Bharata's name, hoping to stir Queen Kaikeyi's maternal feelings. "What about Bharata?" he said desperately. "Do you think he will approve of this? What will he get in return? A fallen father, an estranged brother whom he loves, and a family cast away into the forest. Do you think he will be able to rule in peace, knowing the price paid for his crown? Will he not be haunted by the ghosts of your actions? Can any of this be worth it in the end?"

Queen Kaikeyi stood her ground. She saw the king's hesitation as a betrayal of his promise, a failure unbecoming of his royal line. She even threatened to end her own life if her two demands were not met.

Seeing that she remained unmoved, King Dasharatha realised he was faced with the most difficult decision of his life - one that would tear at his very soul - to either banish his son Rama - whom he loved more than his own life - to the forest for fourteen long years or break the solemn promise he had made, as king, to his queen. From sheer emotional strain, King Dasharatha fainted and lay there on the floor throughout the night as the hours crawled by slowly and ever so treacherously.

This heart-wrenching scene contrasted sharply with the city's lively streets and homes. Unaware of the turmoil within the palace walls, its citizens awoke to a day they believed would be filled with joy and celebration. The streets were alive with colour and festivities. To mark the occasion, Sage Vashishta led a magnificent march through the streets, carrying holy water from the river in a large parade of men and women that formed behind him. As he neared the palace, he sent Sumantra, the minister, to inform the king that all the preparations for the coronation ceremony were complete.

Queen Kaikeyi, unmoved, dismissed the message sent forth by Sage Vashishta and, with an icy demeanour, instructed Sumantra to summon the Rama at once. When Rama arrived, he found his father collapsed in grief, sobbing uncontrollably. King Dasharatha reached out, barely able to speak at the sight of his most beloved son. "Rama... Rama..." he gasped, again and again.

CHAPTER 10

Preparing to Say Goodbye for Fourteen Long Years

QUEEN KAIKEYI TOOK IT UPON HERSELF TO REVEAL TO RAMA THE conditions of the promises she had claimed from the king and what, therefore, was to unfold.

To her surprise, Rama accepted her decision with grace and without the slightest touch of hesitation. He assured Queen Kaikeyi that he would willingly endure any hardship, drown himself in the vast sea, leap into a burning fire, or drink the deadliest of poisons if that was his father's wish. Just as surely, he would gladly go to the forest that very day. Queen Kaikeyi felt smug and satisfied, not fully comprehending the sheer vastness of the tragedy and devastation it would bring down upon all those she held dear, not least upon her own son, Bharata.

Gathered around his father, Rama was both firm and comforting. "Father, you need not despair. It is my solemn duty to honour the promises you have made. I accept this exile willingly. I do not feel wronged, and do not covet the throne. Your honour is what matters most to me. As for the fourteen years, they will pass. Promise me that you will care for my mother during this time, for her heart will ache with my absence. I wish to find her happy and well upon my return."

Deep down, King Dasharatha had harboured a hope, however faint, that Rama would contest, even defy, his unjust demands and assert his rightful claim to the throne. Yet, he understood his son's nature too well - Rama would never disobey his father's word, no matter the personal sacrifice it required.

Amidst this turmoil, Queen Kausalya was consumed by maternal despair. Rama was not just her child but the fulfilment of her deepest prayers, born only after heavenly intervention. "You, the joy of my world, must stay with me in my old age," she pleaded. "I need to have you close to me. Who will bring light to my world as you do?"

Rama, moved by his mother's grief, knelt before her and said gently, "Mother, your sorrow pierces my heart. Every part of me longs to stay by your side, to be the son you need me to be. But please give me your blessings and strength to fulfil my dharma and honour my father's will. Only with your love can I find the courage to walk this path."

Too overwhelmed by grief, Queen Kaushalya struggled to speak.

Rama took her hand warmly. "Will you look after yourself and Father while I am away? You'll need each other's love now more than ever."

As Rama prepared to depart, he urged his wife, Sita, to stay behind and care for his mother. He was reluctant to subject her to the hardships and solitary life of the forest. However, Sita protested, standing firmly by her decision to accompany her husband.

"In joy and in adversity alike, we are bound together," she declared. "Wherever you go, I will go. Just as the sun cannot be parted from its light, nor the river from its flow, I cannot be separated from you. *Jahan Ram, wahan Sita* - wherever there is Rama, there too shall be Sita."

Lakshmana wouldn't give in so easily, either. "This is a great injustice, my brother," he said, his voice ripe with anger. "On what should have been a day of joy and celebration, you are being condemned to the forest for fourteen years. I will not stand idly by while others prey on your misfortune. Let them come - I will challenge anyone who dares oppose you and see your rightful place as king restored."

Rama was all too aware of Lakshmana's fierce affection and strength. "My loving, courageous brother, you are my heart and soul. But remember, whether right or wrong, just or unjust, our highest duty is to fulfil our father's wish and uphold his promise as king. That is our dharma. And what would I do with a kingdom that comes to me against our father's wishes? And of our mother, Queen Kaikeyi - think no ill of her. She has been as loving to us all these years as only a mother can. Her actions are guided by providence; she is but an instrument of that fate, playing her part in destiny's grander designs."

Though his anger cooled, Lakshmana's protective instincts toward his brother only hardened. He made the decision to follow Rama and Sita into exile. Taking his wife Urmila's hands gently, he asked her to remain in Ayodhya to care for their parents.

"Please, let your care for my parents come first, even above your love for me."

In this time of great upheaval and sorrow, Queen Sumithra remained a pillar of strength and light, offering wisdom where grief threatened to take hold.

"Stand by your brother, my son," she told Lakshmana, "as you always have. Nothing matters more right now than remaining at his side now, as his path grows hardest."

To Queen Kaushalya, whose heart ached for Rama's fate, she offered comfort, urging her to see beyond the present pain. "Do not sorrow, dear sister. Look at Rama with pride. He follows his dharma - his sacred duty - for a cause far greater than himself, one that will be remembered for all time. The actions of Rama today will be held in honour by our forebears."

She felt that this moment - this trial of exile and sacrifice - was the beginning of something vast and important. "The lamp which Rama lights today will glow forever. Send him forth, dear Kaushalya, not with tears but with all your strength and blessings."

The kingdom was plunged into mourning when the news of Rama's banishment spread. The once joyful atmosphere gave way to gloom and despair. The playful winds from the day before now held great pain. With rage in their hearts and loss weighing heavily upon them, the citizens cursed Queen Kaikeyi and her actions. Rama, Sita and Lakshmana accepted their exile by replacing their royal robes of silk and gold with simple garments made from the bark of trees. As they departed in their chariot to leave behind their familiar world, the faithful minister Sumantra went with them.

The people of Ayodhya sorrowfully pour

into the streets to follow Rama into exile.

The people of Kosala followed along, running wildly behind the chariot, their wails filling the air as they mourned the departure of the young royals. The whole kingdom seemed to have been flooded with pain and tears.

Rama addressed the crowd, his voice full of compassion. "O beloved citizens of Ayodhya, I entrust my father and each of my mothers to your care and affection. Bless us as we journey into exile, that we may uphold the sacred command of our father and king, and honour his will. I leave Bharata in your hands, to guide and serve you as your sovereign. Remain steadfast, as you have always been - the strength and soul of this great kingdom."

But no words could comfort the grieving people of Kosala, who could not bring themselves to leave. By nightfall, Rama, Sita, and Lakshmana reached the banks of the river Tamasa. While Rama understood the people's anguish, he knew the journey to the forest was one that they had to make alone. Wishing for them to return to the warmth of their homes, and unable to bear the thought of them enduring the forest's hardships, Rama, Sita, and Lakshmana made the heartbreaking decision to slip away quietly, under the cover of nightfall, from Tamasa's edge.

CHAPTER 11

The King Is Dead

RAMA DISPATCHED SUMANTRA TO AYODHYA WITH EXPLICIT INSTRUCTIONS to care for the king. However, Dasharatha, already weakened by Rama's departure, could not bear the heart-wrenching news that his beloved children had already crossed the river and were headed deeper into the forest, away from him for a seemingly endless fourteen years. This proved too wounding for the King. The night echoed with his laments, as his heart ached for his children, until the flames of life - symbolising the strength and glory of the once-mighty king - began to flicker and fade. In a state of inconsolable sorrow, King Dasharatha, the greatest and most beloved ruler of the *Ikshvaku* dynasty, drew his final breath.

The sun sets on Kosala, mirroring the extinguished life of its grief-stricken king.

THE STORY OF SHRAVAN KUMAR AND HIS BLIND PARENTS

King Dasharatha believed that his misfortunes resulted from a curse placed on him by the parents of a young boy named Shravan Kumar. Through fate and misfortune, the boy's life had become intertwined with Dasharatha's.

Shravan Kumar's parents, Shantanu and Malaya, both blind, lived as hermits. Shravan had been a devoted son from a young age, dutifully looking after his ageing parents with great care and affection. As his parents grew older, they expressed their wish to undertake a pilgrimage, a common practice in Hindu culture. Shravan carefully placed each of his parents in a separate basket, which he then fastened to either end of a bamboo pole. He then hoisted this pole onto his shoulders and embarked on the pilgrimage, carrying his beloved parents throughout their sacred journey, serving as their eyes and strength.

Long before he became ruler of Ayodhya, when he was still a young prince, King Dasharatha had gone on a hunt. During this expedition, Prince Dasharatha positioned himself near the riverbank, bow poised, when rippling water caught his attention. Convinced it was a deer drinking from the stream, he released his arrow without a second thought.

But when he crossed the river to claim his prize, lying before him was not a deer, but a young boy, his body trembling in pain. Shravan Kumar - the devoted son - had come to the river to fetch water for his thirsty, blind parents. Dasharatha's arrow had struck him down. In his dying moments, Shravan's voice was steady, even as his breath grew weak. "I do not fear death," he said. "But my parents - my blind, helpless parents - are waiting for me. They will not understand why I do not return. Please... take them water. Tell them what has happened, so they do not suffer the agony of not knowing."

This placed an unbearable burden of grief and guilt upon the prince, yet he shouldered the responsibility of delivering the devastating truth. When Shravan's parents heard of their son's tragic fate, they recognised it as a terrible accident and acknowledged Dasharatha's remorse and compassion. Even as they appreciated Prince Dasharatha's heartfelt gesture of personally informing them, the devastating loss of their beloved child left them too heartbroken to endure the shock.

Unable to imagine a life without their son, they uttered a curse upon Dasharatha, foretelling that he, too, would one day endure the anguish of losing a son. Inconsolable from the blow fate had dealt them, the parents lost their will to live and breathed their last beside their son.

The heartbreaking tale of Shravan Kumar, the dutiful son, and his blind parents.

CHAPTER 12

Building a New Home in Chitrakuta

On the third day, Rama, Sita, and Lakshmana crossed the mighty Ganges. The river's vast expanse and spiritual essence symbolised their passage from the familiar world of Kosala into the untamed realms of the forest.

As they journeyed deeper into the wilderness, they were hit by a sense of unease, for it was true that the desolate forest, even as it held a certain godly mystique, was known to keep demons and dangerous creatures in its midst.

Soon, their path led them to Rishi Bharadwaj, a sage celebrated for his wisdom and deep spiritual insights. Rishi Bharadwaj welcomed his guests warmly and offered them food and shelter at his *ashram*.

The sixth day brought them to Chitrakuta, a secluded sanctuary the sage had recommended. It was here that they met Valmiki.

VALMIKI

The story of Valmiki's transformation from Ratnakar, a feared bandit, to a revered sage and poet is one of the most profound narratives of redemption and spiritual awakening in Hindu tradition.

Revered as the *Adi Kavi* (the first poet) of Sanskrit literature, Valmiki is credited with composing the Ramayana, the first great epic *kavya*, a poem that would shape the moral and spiritual imagination of generations to come.

But he was not always a sage - his wisdom emerged from a darker past.

Valmiki was born in the *Treta Yuga*, an era woven with myth and celestial forces. But his early years were far from divine. He was Ratnakar - a hunter and a bandit, feared by travellers and untouched by morality. He lived by preying upon the innocent, stealing and killing to sustain his family, surviving at the very edges of society and virtue.

One fateful day, Ratnakar attempted to rob a passing sage - none other than Sage Narad. But Narad did not react with anger or fear. Instead, he met the bandit's aggression with kindness. When Ratnakar demanded all that he carried, Narad simply offered him the rag he was wearing. The gesture was so unexpected, so devoid of resistance or hatred, that it unravelled something deep within Ratnakar.

For the first time in his life, he saw himself - not as a feared outlaw, but as a man standing before someone who refused to see him as beyond redemption, but rather as someone deserving a second chance. Shame washed over him. Overcome with emotion, Ratnakar fell to his knees and begged for forgiveness.

Perceiving the sincerity of Ratnakar's remorse, Narad took him under his wing. He instructed Ratnakar to recite the name "Rama" as an act of penance, which Ratnakar faithfully practised for years. His penance was so intense and prolonged that an anthill gradually formed around him. Hence, he earned the name "Val-Miki," which means "one who emerged from an anthill."

His story is a testament to the belief that no one is beyond redemption and that the divine grace of *dharma* is accessible to all who seek it with a true heart.

Valmiki established an *ashram* at that very spot, which would serve as the birthplace of the Ramayana and, in later years, a refuge for Sita and her twin sons, Lava and Kusha.

Chitrakuta, as if peeled from the earth's bosom, was an idyllic paradise alive with the sights and sounds of blooming flowers, tall trees, and cheerful streams; it was filled with birdsong and the playful hum of bees. Rama, Sita, and Lakshmana transformed their simple dwelling into an earthly paradise - not just through the splendid natural beauty surrounding them, but through the deep love binding their hearts.

They lived on the forest's gifts: for food, they relied on its bounty that included fruits, wild roots, leaves, herbs, and berries, and for water, on the pristine streams and natural springs. They built a small hut by the stream, which would shelter them through the changing seasons, and become their home for years to come.

Surrounded by Chitrakuta's tranquil beauty, Rama, Sita, and Lakshmana seek strength and purpose in their ascetic life.

CHAPTER 13

A Kingdom Divided - Bharata's Quest for Redemption

FOLLOWING KING DASHARATHA'S UNTIMELY PASSING, SAGE VASHISHTA sent a courier bearing an urgent summons for Bharata's immediate return to Ayodhya. Bharata and his brother Shatrughna, who had been away at their *nanihal* (maternal grandparents' home), remained unaware of the recent events that had upended the kingdom.

Though the message revealed nothing, its very urgency filled Bharata with dread..

This feeling only grew as he entered the city, puzzled by its unnatural silence. Even the sky looked drained of colour.

His disquiet deepened as he approached the empty palace courtyards, usually filled with bustle and cheer. Upon entering the palace, the sight that greeted him did nothing to take the edge off his apprehensions. Queen Kaikeyi, displaying no emotion, proceeded to explain the situation to him.

"Your father, of great fame, has gone far beyond our mortal realm into the world of the gods. He will eternally watch over you and keep you safe. You are now king and must do his will. The people of Ayodhya await your rule."

Bharata felt a lively pain and rage course through him as his mother revealed the full scope of her treachery.

"I acted out of my love for you," she insisted, her voice tense but firm. "You, above all, should understand why this was necessary."

Bharata stepped back, his voice bitter, "If this is your idea of love, I am sickened by it. Are you truly so blind to the enormity of just what you have done?"

To Bharata, his mother's actions represented the ultimate betrayal. The news of his beloved father's death struck him like a dagger to the heart, choking him with searing pain and guilt. He blamed himself for this turn in their family's fate. He couldn't comprehend how his mother could place the throne above his father's life and his brother's rightful claim to it. He could only conclude that some malevolent force had taken hold of his mother; yet even so, the pain left no room for forgiveness in his heart.

"My head is burning, and my heart feels hot. I can no longer take you as my mother." With these words, he stormed out of the chambers. The grand palace, once a place of such warmth and familiarity, now felt empty and lifeless. Its expansive corridors stretched out before him like an endless maze, haunted by apparitions of the past.

Determined to set things right, Bharata made his way to Queen Kaushalya. She had to know that he had no part in any of this. To his astonishment, Queen Kaushalya received him with boundless love, her motherly affection undimmed by these palace intrigues. She touched his cheek softly and drew him against her. "My darling Bharata," she whispered, "this kingdom and throne are rightfully yours, as your father willed it so. Nothing holds me here anymore. My heart follows Rama, and I long only to join him in the forest." Overcome, Bharata broke down.

Set on correcting this wrong, Bharata set out for the forest to bring Rama home to Ayodhya. He was accompanied by a modest escort that included a small army detachment, priests, ministers, select citizens, and Queen Kaushalya. This assembly comprising those closest to him marked the solemnity of his mission to reinstate Rama as the true King of Kosala.

Meanwhile, deep in the forest, Lakshmana was out hunting when he sensed the earth trembling beneath the thundering hooves of approaching horses. He scaled a tree and, positioning himself for a clearer view, saw an advancing army bearing the royal flag of Ayodhya billowing in the wind. His mind was clouded with suspicion, convinced that Bharata had come to harm them. The hurt from Queen Kaikeyi's betrayal ran deep, and he couldn't help but suspect that Bharata had played his part in the recent betrayal.

"The army draws closer," he exclaimed to Rama in anger and frustration. "And it is led by none other than our villainous brother. What could he possibly want now?"

"Do not rush to judgement, Lakshmana," Rama reproached him gently, "and do not give in to anger. You know well that Bharata is pure and innocent and has a heart of gold. We must not blame him for the burdens that have been thrust upon him. Let us prepare to meet our dear brother, who is now our king - he deserves our welcome, not our scruples."

As Bharata came into view, Lakshmana couldn't help but notice that his brother's once easy smile had vanished; his formerly carefree face now looked worn and tense. In a show of solidarity with his brothers, Bharata had chosen to dress himself in attire made of bark. This unexpected gesture touched Lakshmana's conscience, making him regret the earlier suspicion he had allowed himself to feel toward his younger brother.

Reunited, Bharata embraced his brothers tightly, unwilling to let them go. "My heart will only know joy when you return," he said, his voice choked with emotion. Bharata spoke about his guilt and sorrow over what had happened. "I feel responsible for this tragedy and struggle to accept all that has occurred."

"Say no more, Bharata," Rama interrupted gently, placing a reassuring hand on his brother's face. "You bear no blame in any of this. You are my beloved brother. Fate has chosen this path for all of us, and we must each walk it with courage. Take heart, for these years will pass, and we shall be together again."

Learning of their father's passing, Rama and Lakshmana fell into a grief so deep they could not bring themselves to speak, finding comfort in each other's presence. Once filled with joyous sounds of life, their surroundings now held a funereal quiet.

They selected a sacred spot near their home to offer prayers for their departed father, entrusting their grief to the river's comforting embrace. As the gentle currents whispered past, Sage Vashishta consoled the brothers, "Your father, a king without equal, shall live on eternally within you. Such, my dear children, is the cosmic cycle of life and death to which we are each so inescapably bound."

Bharata, Sage Vashishta, and Queen Kaushalya pressed Rama to reconsider his decision to go into exile. Still, Rama remained staunch, saying that he could not break the word he had given his father. "The trees may shed their leaves, and the sun its shimmer; the oceans may dry up; indeed, the sky may come undone, but my promise to my dear father will remain unbreakable."

Rama then turned to Bharata and urged him to embrace his duty as the king of Kosala. "Honour our father by ruling justly, as I will honour him by keeping my vow of exile."

Rama went on to stress the importance of living by the values of their upbringing - of faithfulness, honour and obedience - now more so than ever before. "If we forsake these values when they're hardest to follow," Rama reflected, "what meaning do they truly hold?"

"Our paths in life are not always of our choosing," he continued. "Indeed, it is not our place to question how we came to be here, for circumstances often come unbidden." He paused, meeting Bharata's eyes. "By staying true to this path, we will find our truest fulfilment." Rama then entrusted Bharata with the care of their mothers and the rest of the family.

Accepting that further pleas would be futile, Bharata made one last request. "At the very least, give me your padukas. I will place them upon the throne as a symbol that I am ruling in your name, and I will await the better days of your return." Moved by his brother's gesture, Rama complied and handed his *padukas* (sandals) to Bharata. Holding them close, Bharata solemnly vowed, "If you do not return after your exile, my dear brother, I swear by these sacred flames that I will enter the fire and end my life."

Bharata pleads for Rama to return to Ayodhya and take his rightful place as king.

Remaining faithful to his pledge, Bharata placed Rama's sandals upon the royal throne, a sign that he was merely a steward of Rama's kingship. In an additional gesture of solidarity, he chose to live not in the grandeur of Ayodhya's palaces but instead moved to the humble village of Nandigram, from where he administered, as Rama's regent, his duties to the people of Kosala.

CHAPTER 14

Life in the Forest

HAUNTED BY MEMORIES THAT REFUSED TO FADE – THOSE TIED TO the arrival of their innocent but distraught brother, the news of their father's passing, and the lingering melancholy in Queen Kaushalya's eyes as she bade them farewell – Rama longed to leave the Chitrakuta forest. Needing distance from these painful reminders, they ventured deeper into the wilderness, eventually finding sanctuary in the remote Dandaka forest.

The forest was unforgiving, and a world away from the comforts of the palace they had once known. Yet, as time passed, Rama, Sita, and Lakshmana adapted to their new life. For Sita, raised in the luxury of a royal household, the hardships of exile could not have been easy. Still, she bore them with quiet grace, never giving way to despair, taking her strength from the love she had for Rama.

This time in the forest wasn't just about survival. Rama, Sita, and Lakshmana grew in wisdom too. They encountered wise sages, attended to and absorbed their teachings, and grasped a deeper understanding of life. Occasionally, they would fight off man-eating demons, earning the blessings and admiration of those they protected.

In this way, the days went on and the months turned into years. After years had passed, with only four years remaining of their exile, they came upon a sage by the name of Sutikshna. Impressed by the princes, he urged Rama to seek the blessings of Sage Agastya, one of the *Sapta Rishis* (Seven Great Sages), whose wisdom was said to surpass that of all others combined.

Seeing something remarkable in them, Sage Agastya searched through his treasures to honour their visit. He then presented Rama with Vishnu's bow and armour, which no weapon could penetrate. He entrusted them with powerful artefacts to help them in their role as protectors. "With these," he told the brothers, "defend the innocent and rid the world of the rakshasas.

He then guided them toward a place called Panchavati, a part of the forest known for its beauty and serenity.

On their way, they came across a majestic vulture resting on the branch of an ancient tree. Its wings stretched wide, catching the golden light of the setting sun. The sight alone was striking, but what truly took them by pleasant surprise was the voice that followed - deep and resonant with human-like clarity.

With a respectful bow, the great bird introduced himself: "I am Jatayu, guardian of these lands and loyal servant to King Dasharatha. His kindness and honour are deep in my memory, and though my wings have aged, I pledge what remains of my strength to you."

Rama leaned forward, his expression softening. "You knew my father?" he asked, captivated by curiosity and wonder.

Jatayu's wise eyes met Rama's. "I knew your father very well indeed," he replied. "Long ago in his youth, while travelling through this very forest, he found me - wounded by a hunter's arrow. Your father didn't turn away. He tended to my injuries, stayed by my side, and saw to it that I recovered to my full strength. Since that day, I have carried his compassion fully in my heart."

Hearing these words, Rama bowed. "To meet someone who carries my father's memory in this way brings me peace."

Sitting beside him, Sita and Lakshmana exchanged glances. Jatayu's noble words and impressive presence offered a sense of reassurance to them. In that moment, Jatayu became more than a new acquaintance and protector - he became instead a living connection to their father's legacy, and a reminder of the enduring ties of *dharma* and devotion - the bonds that transcended time, distance, and circumstance.

CHAPTER 15

Lakshmana Cuts off Shurpanakha's Nose and Ears

RAMA, LAKSHMANA, AND SITA CROSSED THE GODAVARI RIVER AND finally arrived at Panchavati. Panchavati was a place of natural abundance, surrounded by enchanting hills, where birds and animals roamed freely. As they wandered deeper, they stumbled upon a remarkably pristine clearing, untouched by the dark forces known to haunt these woods.

"Let us make our home here in this tranquil haven," Rama suggested. His voice had a newfound peace.

Jatayu, ever the vigilant protector, lived nearby, keeping a protective eye on Sita while the brothers hunted for food.

The peace of their dwelling in Panchavati, however, was deceptive. Before they had left Sage Agastya's *ashram*, he had warned them: "Ravana's sister, Shurpanakha, prowls nearby - and she's more dangerous than any beast you'll encounter." His words clearly hinted at the darker forces the forest concealed.

One day, the very same Shurpanakha caught sight of Rama and, finding him the most handsome man she had ever seen, fell instantly in love. Had Rama seen her true form, he would have beheld something unlike anything he had faced before - her voice sharp and grating, her clawed fingers curled like talons, her fangs jutting past her lips, and her breath reeking of smoke and sulphur.

Yet, despite her repulsive appearance, Shurpanakha possessed the ability to take on any human form. She transformed herself into a strikingly beautiful woman and approached Rama. "If you would have me, my noble prince, I offer myself to you in marriage," she proposed demurely. "Fate has destined us for each other, and I am here to unite with you as your wife."

Upon discovering that Rama was already married to the beautiful Sita, Shurpanakha was filled with dismay. Jealousy consumed her heart at the sight of his wife. She sniffed at Sita, calling her an "insect" and claiming superiority over her. "I could devour her, making way for my union with Rama," she reasoned.

The demoness made big promises to lure Rama. "If we were to wed, my love, my brother Ravana would extend his full protection to you. You would then have nothing to fear from any demon."

With a hint of playfulness, Rama directed her attention to Lakshmana, suggesting she might consider marrying his fine and handsome brother instead.

Lakshmana promptly protested, "I am as much married as my brother, but I thank you all the same."

Shurpanakha grew angry that the brothers were making light of her burning proclamations of love. "I am not to be so easily passed over. You mock me at your peril."

Sensing her mounting anger, Lakshmana attempted to soothe her. "Never mind what my brother Rama says. He means well."

The banter continued in this way for a while, during which Shurpanakha only grew more sullen. She wouldn't give up so easily, however, on the handsome prince. Fired up by resentment, she resolved to eliminate the obstacle she saw in Sita.

She lunged at Sita, but in a flash, Rama pulled Sita away from the attack. At the same time, Lakshmana delivered sharp and decisive strikes with his sword, cutting off Shurpanakha's nose and ears.

To protect Sita, Lakshmana intervenes and cuts off the nose and ears of the demon king's sister.

CHAPTER 16

The Battle Between Rama and Fourteen Thousand Rakshasas

SHURPANAKHA'S AGONISING HOWLS RIPPED ACROSS THE FOREST, SENDing chills through the giant trees. As she fled the scene, her cries reached her cousins, Khara and Dushana - Dandaka's fearsome overlords and commanders of legions of demons. They were sworn guardians of Ravana's sister, and anger coursed hot through their blood as they vowed retaliation against those responsible for her suffering.

"Avenge this humiliation," Shurpanakha demanded of them, still in excruciating distress.

"Do not be troubled, our dear Shurpanakha," they replied. "Those responsible for this dishonour will soon face their reckoning."

Trailing the scent of human flesh, Khara, Dushana, their generals, and their demon army advanced towards Rama and Lakshmana, thirsting for their blood. Lakshmana could sense the disturbance. He glanced skyward to see it darken and overrun with a swarm of flying demons. "Brother," he said with unease, "something dire approaches." The winds howled, and the turbulent and menacing skies roiled above them as clouds gathered, ready to burst. A demonic horde descended in chariots pulled by snarling beasts, horses, and elephants, their purpose deadly and clear.

In a spectacular display of supreme strength,

Rama annihilates the legion of fourteen thousand rakshasas.

Rama directed Lakshmana to escort Sita to safety and guard her closely.

He then steeled himself, turning his attention to the vast and rapidly advancing army of demons. Their approach was marked by the deafening beat of drums and the savage cries of battle. It was evident they were driven by their only desire - to wreak utter death and destruction.

One of the demons, who appeared to be their leader, strode forward and, blazing with anger, declared, "Know we are here to avenge the harm you perpetrated on our sister. Be prepared to perish."

Standing alone against the vast army, Rama tried to reason with them, but quickly realised the *rakshasas* only wanted bloodshed.

"You quake in fear of our mighty army," one of the demons mocked. "It is the coward who seeks to talk his way out of fear."

Khara and Dushana exchanged glances, expecting Rama to cower at the sight of their imposing army. Instead, Rama stood still, unmoved. "If battle is what you seek, then battle you shall have," he said calmly. Then, with a silent prayer to the heavens - for strength, and for forgiveness for what he must do - he stepped forward to face them.

With a commanding look towards the sky, Rama opened fire. Each arrow, fiery and unerring, struck like a blaze of the sun. The mortally wounded demons fell to the earth like giant flies. Rama finally confronted Dushana and Khara, condemning them for the years of death and destruction they had wrought upon the forests and for the countless innocent lives mercilessly taken in their wake.

Ultimately, with unmatched skill, Rama wielded his weapon to single-handedly defeat not just Dushana and Khara but nearly all fourteen thousand demon warriors they had brought with them to the battle that night.

CHAPTER 17

Ravana Thirsts for Revenge

BLOODIED AND SHAKEN, AKAMPANA - AMONG THE FEW RAKSHASAS to survive the slaughter - fled to Lanka, bearing the grim news of their clash with Rama in the Panchavati forest.

"O, mighty king! I am mortified that a mere human has slain Khara and Dushana. Their entire force, fourteen thousand strong, also lie slain!" Ravana stared at him in disbelief. He clenched his jaw as he contemplated the nature of sorcery that could destroy so many of his warriors in a single blow. So consumed was he with rage that he vowed revenge against the gods themselves, threatening to burn the God of Fire and choke the God of Wind.

Ravana's anger flared even further at the appearance of his sister, Shurpanakha, her disfigured face bearing the full agony and humiliation she had endured.

Shurpanakha spun a captivating image of Sita, her voice dripping with a mix of admiration and cunning. "Her beauty is beyond compare, my dear brother," she said. "She glows with a light that is unmatched by any mortal. She will be a queen like no other, the most radiant jewel in your crown." In this way, Shurpanakha sought to weave a spell of enchantment around Sita's image crafted to stoke Ravana's desires as much as to settle her own scores for the indignities she had just suffered.

Despite his heart seething with rage from the loss of his kin and army, Ravana found himself consumed by Shurpanakha's conjuring. The prospect of making a woman of such beauty his queen - and the challenge it touched off - inflamed both his vanity and his conqueror's instinct.

"I must lay eyes on Sita myself then," Ravana declared. "If she is indeed as exquisite as you say she is, then surely she is fated to be mine, and mine alone."

"I tried to seize her for you, my brother," Shurpanakha snarled, "but that cowardly Lakshmana ambushed me, and look - this is the result." She gestured to her mutilated face.

"You must avenge my honour for what they have done, avenge the slaughter of *rakshasas* whose spirits now roam restlessly, demanding retribution."

Listening intently to the discussions and recognising Rama's apparent invincibility, Akampana proposed a cunning plan.

"The surest path to revenge," he suggested, "is to strike at Rama through his beloved Sita. Without her, he would surely die of a broken heart."

Ravana, his mind already entranced by visions of Sita's beauty, was now excited by the scheme's prospects. Applauding Akampana's genius, he saw the plot as the perfect justification to mask his true intent - which was to abduct Sita so he could make her his wife. His heart raced with anticipation, not so much at the thought of avenging his sister's humiliation or retaliating for the fallen *rakshasas* but rather at the tantalising prospect of claiming the beautiful princess as his queen.

In this delirious state, Ravana set off, for the first time in our story, for a direct confrontation with Rama.

Our readers must note that, though he may appear maniacal, Ravana was no ordinary adversary. A titan of demonic strength and intellect, he was renowned as the most powerful *rakshasa* ever to live. Ravana possessed not just unmatched physical might but also demonstrated remarkable scholarly ability through his deep knowledge of the *Vedas*. His ten heads and twenty arms were not mere grotesque excesses but symbols of uncommon knowledge, strength, and dominion over the body and mind. Though he had descended into tyranny, Ravana was no common oppressor. He remained one of Lord Shiva's greatest devotees and an unstoppable warrior, whose terror reached all three worlds. He had proven his battle skills for over a thousand years such that his victories had taken the form of legend. Such was his devotion and might that he earned the rarest of blessings - near immortality granted by Lord Brahma and Lord Shiva themselves.

But it was also true that his achievements were marred by his supreme arrogance and ruthless brutality.

Ravana called for his magical chariot, the *Pushpaka Vimana*, and swiftly departed to execute his most brazen plans.

After tearing through vast oceans and soaring over high mountains, he arrived at Maricha's hut. The great magician also happened to be his uncle and the same son of Tataka whom, earlier in the story, Rama cast into the sea.

Though Maricha belonged to the demon race, he had been seeking to repair the ways of his past and pursue a life of virtue since that day Rama had spared his life. He cautioned Ravana against provoking the young prince, but Ravana was not in the mood to listen to reason or restraint.

"What reckless foolishness grips you, Ravana?" Maricha scolded him. "What has come over you - to be so besotted by another man's wife, whom you have never even laid eyes on, much less know? You are inviting certain doom for yourself and your people." But Ravana would hear nothing of it.

Maricha, now wise and wary, posed an alternative. "If you are this intent on taking revenge, why not challenge Rama to a fair fight instead?"

Ravana scoffed. "He is a worthless nobody, banished from his own kingdom and reduced to a hermit's existence in the forest. I will not lower myself to fight such a wretch."

"Rama is far from ordinary," Maricha countered forcefully. "He is certainly not just some wretch as you say he is. Think about it. What mere mortal can single-handedly kill fourteen thousand of our demons or, as only a young boy, defeat the fiercest Tataka? He had the power to take my life, yet chose mercy. You have everything - a life of incomparable enjoyment, a prosperous kingdom, and power beyond anyone's reckoning. Are you this determined to go out of your way to pursue certain destruction and death?"

But Ravana was so possessed by his desires that he remained deaf to all reason.

Maricha offered a final warning, "This path will only lead Lanka to ashes and cause the end of the rakshasa race."

Ravana's mind was closed. Ravana knew that Maricha's powers could allow him to assume any form, human or beast. To Ravana then, Maricha was merely an instrument to be used in accomplishing his grand plans. Ravana threatened Maricha with death if he did not cooperate. Maricha realised the futility of resistance and, therefore, found himself with no choice but to agree to help his nephew.

Together thus, they set off towards the Panchavati forest.

CHAPTER 18

The Illusion and the Capture - Rama and Lakshmana are Tricked

THE PLAN WAS SET IN MOTION.

In the serene expanse of Panchavati, amid the soft murmur of the gentle stream and the chirping of birds, Sita was gathering blossoms as she often did, finding comfort in nature's embrace. As she moved from one bloom to another, a sudden rustle caught her attention. A deer emerged from the thicket, capturing her gaze. Its golden coat glistened under the sun's rays, and its spots glinted like tiny diamonds, a sight so breathtaking as to be otherworldly. The deer frolicked into the clearing before pausing to nibble on the lush grass. It then disappeared briefly, only to return and affectionately lock eyes with Sita.

The deer's presence tugged at Sita's heart. She turned to Rama. "Look at its gentle eyes and graceful movements. Have you ever seen anything so enchanting?"

Sita was clearly hypnotised by its form and playfulness. She desired to have the deer as a pet.

Always vigilant and intuitive, Lakshmana studied the creature closely and felt troubled. As if guided by a murmur from the passing breeze, Lakshmana expressed his doubts, "Beware the golden deer, for beauty often masks treachery most foul. There's something disquieting about its perfection, too faultless to be of this world. It would be wise to stay alert."

Torn between his brother's caution and the unmistakable joy it would bring to Sita, Rama observed the deer intently. "Lakshmana, your apprehension reflects wisdom, yet it is difficult to turn away from a creature of such harmless joy. Perhaps we might try to capture it and see. If it proves to be an illusion or trick, we will release it."

Rama pauses to look at the mystical deer, torn between the danger Lakshmana warns of and the delight it would bring to Sita.

Seldom did Sita ask for anything, and Rama found it impossible to refuse her this simple happiness.

So, in a fit of love, he chased after the deer. Soon, he found himself being lured deeper and deeper into the forest, away from the safety of their hut. Before venturing further, he called out to Lakshmana to remain with Sita and protect her at any cost.

When Rama's arrow struck, it was not meant to kill the deer but to subdue it in order to unravel its true nature. As the arrow found its mark, the golden deer's form began to shimmer and contort, finally revealing it to be the demon Maricha. Rama felt a wave of dread as he realised the extent of the deception.

Even as Maricha was losing his life, he mustered the last of his strength for one final act of deceit. In a voice chillingly indistinguishable from Rama's, he cried out in agony, "Lakshmana, come quickly! I need you! O Lakshmana! You must hurry!" Seeing through Maricha's plot, Rama was gripped by dread. He knew exactly what was happening. This was a trap - not for him, but for Sita.

"If Lakshmana heeds the call for help and goes to his rescue, what will happen to Sita, who would be left alone and unprotected?" he thought to himself.

Hearing what she believed to be Rama's call for help, Sita became anxious and pleaded with Lakshmana to hurry to his brother's side.

"Rama is in danger!" she gasped. "You must go to him right away, Lakshmana! He needs you!"

Lakshmana tried to comfort her: "Sita, please remain calm. That voice is nothing but a rakshasa's deception. It cannot be Rama's. There is no peril that Rama cannot overcome. But leaving you alone - that would be a far greater danger, and one my conscience will not allow. He demanded a vow from me to remain beside you no matter what happens."

But Sita was entirely inconsolable by now. She did not accept Lakshmana's assurances and grew increasingly anxious about Rama's safety. "Do not worry about me, Lakshmana," she pleaded. "Look, there is nothing to be afraid of here. Should something happen to Rama, I shall never be able to forgive myself. Please, for my sake, listen to me - your brother needs you now."

CHAPTER 19

Sita is Kidnapped

As SITA'S WORRY FOR RAMA'S SAFETY BORDERED ON FRENZY, SHE became increasingly adamant that Lakshmana go after him, growing so distraught that she even threatened to set herself on fire if he refused. "Do not fret over me; I will be safe," she assured him again, mentioning that Jatayu, the noble bird, would protect her.

Lakshmana was torn between his duty to protect Sita and his obligation to heed her feverish pleas. After a period of tortured hesitation, he yielded ever so reluctantly.

But before setting off, he took a crucial precaution. He traced a protective circle around the hut's entrance and said to Sita, "Wait here, and I will return with Rama. Whatever happens, do not step outside this circle. As long as you remain within its bounds, no harm will come to you." Sita nodded, crossing her arms tightly, her unease growing. She watched Lakshmana grasp his bow and arrows and hurry in the direction of Rama's voice. Even though Sita was the one who insisted that Lakshmana leave, her eyes were wide with worry for him as she watched him disappear into the forest.

Ravana observed their activities from behind a tree where he had been hiding all along. As the events progressed exactly according to his plan, Ravana's satisfaction grew. Upon his first glimpse of Sita, he became even more enchanted by her ethereal beauty, and his desire to carry out his wicked scheme only intensified.

Ravana, disguised as an ascetic, tempts Sita beyond Lakshmana's protective circle.

Seizing his chance in the moments following Lakshmana's departure, Ravana approached Sita under the guise of an old *sanyasi* (ascetic), complete with a begging bowl and staff. In a gesture of respect to the old ascetic, Sita offered him some fruits. However, Ravana, keenly aware of the protective circle drawn by Lakshmana, knew he had to coax Sita to step out of its boundary.

"I am but a sanyasi," he said, adopting a tone of humility. "As a simple hermit, I cannot cross the threshold of your home. It is upon you to step outside for me to graciously accept your offering."

Sita hesitated. Lakshmana's warning was ringing in her mind, as she stood there unwilling to breach the protective circle. Ravana sensed her dilemma and feigned offence, turning away as though slighted. "Ah, what use is the hospitality of one who doubts the sincerity of a sanyasi?" he muttered under his breath but loud enough for Sita to hear. Troubled by the thought of disrespecting an ascetic, and unable to bear the guilt of withholding an offering to one she believed holy, Sita finally stepped outside the protective circle to hand him the fruits.

This was just the moment Ravana had been waiting for. Dropping his disguise, he revealed his true *rakshasa* form and grabbed her wrist. "Come with me and be my queen in Lanka. You shall live a life of unimaginable luxury away from this dreadful place."

Sita winced, startled and furious by this deceit. "Leave at once! My Rama will not tolerate this," she warned.

Ignoring her protests, Ravana forcibly grabbed Sita and pulled her into his chariot. As the chariot ascended into the sky towards Lanka, Sita's cries rang loud, calling desperately for Rama and Lakshmana.

CHAPTER 20

The Valour of the Vulture King

As Ravana whisked Sita away, the tranquility of Panchavati was shattered by the sudden upheaval. The chariot cut a path through the southern skies, catching the attention of Jatayu, who had been resting on a nearby tree. Stirred by the distressing sight of Sita's abduction, he spread his massive wings and flew toward the flying chariot. "I am Jatayu, King of the Vultures," he said as he drew closer. "As a king to another, I demand that you release Sita at once."

Ravana, unimpressed, shot back, "Begone, old bird, while you can, and live out the rest of your days in peace."

Jatayu was undaunted. "To steal another man's wife befits no true king."

Ravana scoffed, "My patience wears thin, old bird. Don't tell me I didn't try to warn you. Now, you will feel my wrath."

Unfazed, Jatayu retorted, "Justice will prevail, and it will be fitting. I will not flinch in bringing about your end."

Ravana brushed off Jatayu's threats. But Jatayu, embodying the ferocity of his species, swooped down like a fiery comet, igniting the skies with his descent, his powerful beak and talons ready for battle. With a mighty strike, he tore off one of the chariot's railings. Doing so freed Sita from the chariot's clutches, and he gently carried her back to the safety of the ground.

The noble vulture Jatayu challenges the demon king

to fend off his brazen attempt to kidnap Sita.

Ravana and Jatayu then clashed in a menacing battle. Jatayu pounced on Ravana, tearing off one of his arms and heads with his powerful talons.

From below, Sita watched in horror as this fierce duel unfolded. Amidst the chaos, she grabbed a piece of her jewellery and discreetly dropped it to the ground, leaving a clue for Rama to follow.

Blood spurted from Ravana's mutilated body, but his severed limbs and head regenerated as swiftly as they had been sundered.

As the intensity of the fight escalated, the brave and glorious Jatayu found himself at his limits, beginning to feel the weight of his years. Sensing this moment of weakness, Ravana drew his sword and, with a ruthless stroke, cut off Jatayu's wings.

The mighty eagle fell to the ground, defeated.

Sita rushed to his side and tenderly caressed the noble bird, whispering words of gratitude. At that moment, however, Ravana grabbed and dragged her back into his chariot. As they rose into the darkened sky once more, the chariot left behind a luminous trail, marking the route to Lanka.

Meanwhile, Lakshmana reunited with Rama, and was relieved to see him unharmed. But Rama was perplexed to see him there. "Lakshmana, my brother, where is Sita? Why have you left her alone?"

Lakshmana recounted the events that had transpired, including Sita's spiralling distress, her unsettling insistence that he respond to what she was certain was Rama's cry for help, and finally, her dramatic threat to end her life.

Anxiously, the two rushed back to their hut, only to find it empty. They searched every nook and corner, calling out Sita's name as loudly as they could, but all in vain.

Rama found himself in the grips of dread and despair, such as he had never felt before. "Sita is not here. Have the demons taken her? Oh, the anguish she must be enduring!"

He buried his face in his hands, weak and delirious from grief. "Could she be hiding behind a tree, playing a joke on us? She must be!" His mind reeled as he pleaded with Lakshmana, "Can you interrogate the trees, plants, deer, or elephants? Perhaps they have witnessed something or know of her whereabouts."

Lakshmana tried to calm his brother down, but Rama was utterly distraught with guilt. "By my life, where is she?! I have failed to protect my wife. What good am I?"

Lakshmana tried to steer his brother away from despair. "Every moment we linger in grief is a moment lost, my brother," he said.

As the brothers began their search, they came upon the gravely wounded Jatayu. The once majestic eagle lay feebly, barely clinging to life, his breathing faint, his strength nearly gone. Rushing to his side, the brothers attentively listened as Jatayu detailed the distressing truth. His voice trembled as he spoke, "It was the demon king, Ravana, who took Sita. I regret I couldn't fend him off."

With hearts heavy yet full of gratitude, Rama and Lakshmana knelt beside Jatayu and held him close.

"You who gave your life to protect Sita," Rama whispered tenderly. "This is a debt we can never repay. Your courage, your sacrifice - this will live in our hearts forever." A faint calm passed over Jatayu's face. Surrounded by the brothers in his final moments, he appeared at peace - comforted in knowing he had fulfilled his *dharma* to the very end.

With tears in their eyes, Rama and Lakshmana remained at his side. They mourned not just a fallen ally but someone who had stood by them without hesitation, with nothing but love and loyalty in his heart.

CHAPTER 21

Hanuman and the Kingdom of the Vanaras

THE BROTHERS, NOW MORE DESPERATE THAN EVER, WERE DETERmined to find Sita. They pushed deeper into the wild, unruly woodlands, where trees towered like silent sentinels. As they traversed the verdant underbrush, the branches seemed to murmur secrets, perhaps warning them of the wild and unforgiving paths ahead. Then something unusual happened - something massive shifted in the shadows. A terrifying, formless creature suddenly emerged, dragging itself towards them. The beast's enormous frame crept forward like a predator on the prowl, with a gaping mouth where its head should have been, and a single, unblinking eye staring out from its chest. Though it possessed no feet, its long, serpent-like arms slithered forward, reaching hungrily to ensnare and crush the princes.

This was Kabandha, a name spoken in fear in these forests. His hunts followed no method or logic; he killed randomly without exceptions - humans and tigers and bears too. He was called the predator who served no master and showed no mercy.

The fight was as fierce as either of them had ever had to face. The princes stood their ground and fought bravely even as the beast battled with seemingly volcanic power. In this manner, the clash continued into the day. Finally, Rama was able to cut off both the demon's arms at once with one decisive blow.

Then, something unexpected happened. Kabandha spoke with a divine calm, revealing a pain that felt deeper than rage. "I wasn't always like this before," he confessed. "I wasn't always…this abominable."

He disclosed his long-buried truth - he had once been a celestial being, cursed into this unsightly form by the gods.

"The prophecy says my suffering will end only when my body burns, when fire consumes what I've become," he explained, his voice eerily calm, but heavy with a long, ancient pain.

Rama looked at the monster and saw past its hideous face to the trapped soul within. Moved by mercy and his understanding of the deeper cosmic order that governed such curses, he honoured Kabandha's final wish. In so doing, he allowed the flames to consume Kabandha's long-persecuted soul, freeing his spirit simultaneously from its demonic bondage. As the fire caught and climbed, Kabandha's misshapen body blackened, then crumbled away. No longer a demon, he rose to his true form - as a radiant, celestial being.

Kabandha, so filled with gratitude, wanted to help the brothers.

"Find Sugriva," he told them. "The monkey king living in exile. Though you don't know it yet, he holds the key. Your paths are destined to cross, and when they do, he'll help you find Sita when no one else can."

Released from his curse and finally at peace, Kabandha ascended to the heavens in a golden chariot, achieving *moksha* (the ultimate liberation of the soul).

Rama and Lakshmana set out for the hills in search of the *vanara* (forest-beings) king Sugriva. Along the way, Lakshmana sought to ease his brother's despair, lifting his spirits with gentle reassurances.

The kingdom of Kishkindha, ruled by the mighty *vanaras*, stretched across dense forests and rugged hills. Its exiled leader, Sugriva, had taken refuge in the city of Rishyamukha, a stronghold on the outskirts, where he and his loyal companions lived in uneasy exile. Among them was Hanuman, son of the Wind God and Sugriva's most devoted follower.

As Rama and Lakshmana neared, Hanuman approached them with an inquisitive eye. "Declare your lineage," he stated. "Your clothes are simple, yet your bearing is noble. You carry the countenance of gods, yet you walk these lands like ascetics. Who are you, and what brings you to these secluded woods?"

Rama and Lakshmana revealed their identities, quickly recounting the tale of their exile, the abduction of Sita, and events up to their encounter with Kabandha. Hanuman listened intently, his keen mind absorbing every detail. He was struck by their humility, despite the godlike aura about them. Hanuman felt an immediate connection with the two brothers, as if destiny had intertwined their paths for a greater cause.

"Come," Hanuman said, "I will carry you upon my shoulders for an audience with Sugriva." Hanuman bore the two princes aloft, leaping across valleys and treetops until they reached the summit of Mount Rishyamukha.

There, standing before them, was Sugriva.

As his eyes fell upon the brothers, Sugriva felt deeply humbled that the noble and virtuous Rama had sought his help. He looked on them worshipfully and beheld in awe the celestial halo cast on these hills by the princes' presence.

Yet beneath their divine radiance, Sugriva glimpsed something familiar - a shadow of sorrow that mirrored his own pain.

"I, too, bear the weight of exile," Sugriva confided to the brothers, his voice full of melancholy.

CHAPTER 22

The Tragic Story of Two Brothers

"IT ALL BEGAN," SUGRIVA SAID, HIS VOICE A WHISPER OF DESPAIR, "WHEN a demon fled and sought refuge in a dark cave. I stood guard at the entrance as my older brother, Vali, chased the demon into the cave's shadowy depths. Before long, eerie cries echoed from within, and a slow trickle of blood began to stain the earth beneath my feet. My heart raced with dread because each drop felt like a death knell."

Believing his brother dead, Sugriva placed a massive boulder to seal the cave's entrance to trap the demon inside and returned to Kishkindha. With Vali dead, the kingdom passed to Sugriva - the crown and, by tradition, Vali's wife Tara, both responsibilities he accepted reluctantly.

"Days later, when Vali emerged alive, he viewed my decisions as calculated treason," Sugriva continued.

"So, you, my own blood, coveted my throne," Vali roared, his eyes aflame.

In a fit of rage, Vali attempted to kill Sugriva and take his wife, Ruma, as his own as further punishment for the perceived treachery. Narrowly escaping, Sugriva sought refuge on Rishyamukha Mountain - the one place Vali could not enter due to a *rishi's* curse.

Sugriva continued, his shoulders heavy with the burden of exile. "For years, I have lived here in fear, banished from my own home, watching as

Vali rules Kishkindha with unchallenged power and cruelty. Every day, I brace for the moment he finds a way to break the curse and destroy me."

"But today," Sugriva said, his voice gaining strength, "I will no longer hide. With your help, I will face him and reclaim everything he took from me. Fate has caused our paths to cross."

Sugriva then reached into his garment. "Look what I found." He stretched out his hand and presented the ornaments Sita had dropped in her struggle with the demon king during her abduction.

Rama wept as he recognised the ornaments. Overcome with emotions, he vowed, "I will restore you to your throne and reunite you with your beloved wife, Ruma."

The group travelled to a mountain in Kishkindha, where Sugriva challenged Vali to a fight. Rama, concealed from view, observed the fight between Vali and Sugriva. Vali, born by the grace of Indra, the God of Thunder, possessed a golden necklace granting him immeasurable strength. There was no doubt that Vali was amongst the mightiest beings that ever lived; legend had it that he had once even defeated Ravana in a fight.

With Rama's help, Sugriva challenges his brother Vali to reclaim his lost honour and the kingdom of Kishkindha.

In the climax of the violent duel between the brothers, Vali, evidently superior in strength, appeared on the verge of victory. To fulfil his vow to Sugriva, Rama released an arrow that pierced Vali's heart, fatally wounding him.

As he lay dying, Vali's eyes, holding both pain and bewilderment, found Rama. "Why, noble prince?" he gasped, blood staining his lips. "What quarrel did you have with me? I have done you no wrong."

His voice grew stronger with indignation despite his weakening body. "You, who bear the great name of Raghu's lineage is this how you honour your ancestors? Striking from hiding like a common assassin?"

Moved by compassion, Rama gently cradled Vali, his own eyes burdened with sorrow. "Brother Vali, forgive me for the pain this brings you. My actions were guided not by hostility, but by dharma itself."

He paused, choosing his words carefully. "I gave my sacred word to Sugriva, who came to me broken and wronged. To restore justice, I was bound by my dharma, my duty to act."

The complexity of their tumultuous past burdened Sugriva, and he felt broken watching his warrior brother's life slip away. In a heartfelt gesture, he vowed to look after his brother's son, Angada, and anoint him crown prince, ensuring his rightful place in the kingdom. In a final mark of reconciliation, Vali bestowed upon Sugriva the necklace given to him by Indra, assigning all its power to him. He also urged his son, Angada, to let go of bitterness and accept Sugriva as his new king with a full heart.

This marked the beginning of a powerful alliance between Rama and Sugriva. Sugriva committed his army, with Hanuman at the forefront, to Rama's cause. Together, they swore eternal friendship over a sacred fire.

Unfortunately, their plans were disrupted by the arrival of the monsoon season. The seas became rough, making it impossible for the company to undertake its mission to Lanka. They were forced to take shelter in a cave and wait for the wet weather to clear. To Rama, the lashing rains seemed like the tears of the gods, mourning his separation from Sita. The sad song in his heart echoed from the Kishkindha mountains to the vast sea and back.

At last, the month of *Kartik* (October) arrived, and as the rain eased, it ushered in clearer skies and calmer seas.

CHAPTER 23

Searching for Sita in Every Corner of the Earth

Under Sugriva's command, four distinct search parties were assembled, each bound for one of the four reaches of the Earth. With no definitive clue of where Sita might be held captive, they were instructed to comb through every conceivable hiding place: under rocks, through forests, across oceans and deserts, along lakes and streams, over sweeping countryside, within ancient forts, down steep gorges, up towering hills, and atop majestic mountains.

Heading southward was the search party led by Angada, the valiant son of Vali. Among its ranks were two of its most formidable members - Hanuman and Jambavana, the wise and ancient king of the bears. Jambavana was no ordinary being; he was said to have been born from the very breath of Brahma when the creator deity exhaled.

Their journey took them to Mahendra Hill, perched on the southern shore of India. There, they encountered Sampati, the elder brother of Jatayu, the noble vulture king. Though time had aged him, and his wings bore the scars of a past attempt to soar too close to the sun, his sight remained astoundingly sharp, allowing him to perceive even distant objects with unparalleled clarity.

Sampati looked across the vast ocean at Hanuman's behest and revealed what he saw. Sita was being held captive in what looked like a fort on a deserted island; she could be seen shedding tears while scores of *rakshasis* stood guard at a watchful distance.

As Angada's group contemplated the enormity of the challenge, Jambavana, the wise bear, reminded Hanuman of a power his father had gifted him: the ability to fly. Despite this power, Hanuman doubted himself and did not feel confident about crossing such a vast ocean.

Sensing his hesitation, Jambavana said, "You are the son of the God of Wind, and your strength exceeds all of us combined. Why do you waver? Do you not realise your true power? Go forth with unflappable confidence so that we may rescue Sita and bring glory to the vanaras."

To further encourage Hanuman, Jambavana recounted an extraordinary tale from his childhood: "As a child, your spirit knew no bounds. Once, you leapt towards the sun to pluck it, mistaking it for a giant ripe fruit. Such audacity startled Indra, the King of Gods, who had to strike you with a thunderbolt in his urgency to protect the sun. This blow wounded you gravely and caused your father, Vaayu, the God of Winds, to halt his breath, smothering all forms of life on earth.

Remember, Hanuman, the wind is vital, sustaining the breath of life itself. To placate your father, the gods not only healed your wounds but also endowed you with celestial gifts. Blessed by Brahma and Indra, you were granted incomparable strength and the unique destiny to meet your end by your own will alone. Now is the time for you to embrace your power and destiny and help our Rama in his quest."

While Hanuman was aware of his divine heritage, he had never faced a challenge that demanded the full realisation of his abilities.

Hanuman thought kindly of Rama, who he knew was beside himself with worry. Determined to help, he expanded his body to an awe-inspiring size. With the newfound confidence that Jambavana had rekindled in him, Hanuman drew a deep, fortifying breath and, with the force of the wind, sprang skyward towards Lanka.

Below, the monkey army erupted in cheers, and even the gods looked on with approval, their smiles blessing Hanuman's path. This leap was to be the first of many of Hanuman's legendary exploits. Alongside Lakshmana, he would take his place as one of Rama's most faithful confidants.

CHAPTER 24

Through Enemy Lines - The Adventures of Hanuman in Lanka

HANUMAN HAD TO OVERCOME NUMEROUS OBSTACLES TO GET TO Lanka. He flew over mystical mountains, outwitted a cunning serpent goddess, and even slew an evil sea monster that came to stand in his path.

When Hanuman alighted in Lanka, he could not help but be awestruck by its glow and grandeur. From atop Mount Trikuta, he beheld a full view of the city below which boasted magnificent palaces alongside enchanting gardens and formidable fortresses. Yet, despite its outward grandeur, Hanuman knew the city's foundations were sullied by plunder and the spoils of war.

As Hanuman surveyed the city's elaborate security arrangement, he saw that it was an unassailable fortress; to breach its walls would be impossible with the city guarded at every turn by vigilant, well-armed sentinels. Doubt crept into his thoughts, and he contemplated the futility of his mission. Had he journeyed this far merely to discover an impossible task? Should he simply turn back? Was all of this in vain?

But he then quickly reminded himself of the mission's significance and chided himself for lacking self-confidence. To elude detection, Hanuman shrank to a diminutive size and snuck into the city under the veil of night. His presence did not go unnoticed, however. The vigilant guardian spirit of Lanka detained him and demanded he identify himself. Maintaining his disguise, Hanuman responded, "I am but a harmless vanara of no threat or consequence to you. I appear to have lost my way; mere chance has led me here."

Hanuman felt something forceful strike him. It was the spirit.

Though momentarily startled by the blow, Hanuman gathered himself before long and returned the attack with a powerful strike of his own.

The spirit was taken aback by Hanuman's unexpected retaliation and found herself thrown off balance by the blow's impact. It wasn't so much the physical pain from the forceful strike that shook her but the recollection of an ancient prophecy. Being struck with such force by a *vanara* had been foretold as an omen of the ultimate destruction of Lanka. The spirit realised the kingdom's days were numbered; Ravana's sins inflicted over all of creation through the years were finally catching up with the fate of his kingdom.

A chilling howl from a pack of wolves perforated the air as if to confirm the omen. Recognising the kingdom's inescapable fate, the spirit said, "Trust not the beauty of Lanka, for it hides a thousand sins. The flames of Lanka shall be the pyre of its king's pride." She stepped aside to allow Hanuman to continue his mission unobstructed.

Hanuman dodged his way quietly into the palace and combed through every chamber. The sheer extravagance left him unsettled. Everywhere he turned, he encountered an abundance of merriment, feasting, and revelry, with not a hint of restraint. Despite the visible extravagance, the city seemed hollow and without solace.

There was no sign of Sita anywhere within the palace walls. Hanuman desperately scoured each corner of the sprawling palace gardens but was unsuccessful. Just as he was about to lose hope, he spotted a pristine white temple nestled within another high-walled garden. In stark contrast to the rest of the palace, the temple suggested a promise of serenity and maybe, just maybe, a clue to Sita's whereabouts.

CHAPTER 25

A Glimmer of Hope

THERE, AMIDST A GROVE OF ASHOKA TREES, A SOLITARY FIGURE rested - a vision of such breathtaking beauty that even though she appeared weary, she looked like a monument to the goddess of beauty herself. Sita was closely watched by a group of hideous *rakshasis* armed with spears, sickles, and swords. One *rakshasi* had no eyes, the other had no nose, and the third was a balding dwarf. Still others bore faces twisted into the grotesque likenesses of oxen and snakes. Sita's soft weeping hung in the air, each tear bearing her heartache.

Hanuman's heart sank with sorrow for the tormented princess. Sita's voice, tender yet full of anguish, repeatedly uttered, "Rama, Rama," as the grief of being apart from her beloved husband pressed heavily upon her.

Hanuman's sorrow soon gave way to overwhelming joy and relief as the significance of his discovery took hold. "I have found Sita. I have found Sita at last!" He could hardly contain his excitement. "I cannot wait to take this news to Lord Rama. This will gladden his heart and bring him the greatest joy."

Just as he was about to approach Sita, he spotted Ravana making his way towards her. The demon king seated himself on the ground beside her. Hanuman hid within earshot to hear what Ravana would say.

"My beautiful Sita, come live with me. Live in my palace and become my most beloved queen. I will grant your every desire. I will surrender command of all three worlds to you." In a voice that was low but insistent, Ravana continued to assert his love, boasting of the immeasurable wealth and power he could offer her. Yet, for Sita, his presence was repulsive; her heart loathed the very sight of him.

"Your words cause me great distress," Sita responded. "I will say it again. You, who have abducted me, have shown yourself to be nothing but a coward and a disgrace. I am the progeny of Mother Earth herself, Rama's beloved wife, the treasured daughter of my father, King Janaka, the honoured daughter-in-law of King Dasharatha, the King of Kings. Rama will come for me and reclaim my honour. Why invite ruin upon yourself and your people?" she reasoned. "Have you not gotten a measure of Rama's strength already? Seek his forgiveness, for he is merciful. Release me now, and he may yet spare your life."

Ravana looked visibly shaken by Sita's pointed, unflinching rebuke. "I am Ravana, a descendant of Lord Brahma himself. Can you not treasure my affection? Would it not be within your heart to love me in return? And what of this Rama? Why do you sing his praises so?"

Sita replied, "Don't you see? Your lineage doesn't concern me. I live and die by Rama."

Ravana's eyes went bloodshot at her snub as he spoke, "I have waited too long for you to keep singing the praise of a worthless, beggarly hermit cast out by his own family and who roams aimlessly, living a beggar's pitiful existence. Be sensible and become my queen. Rama cannot cross the ocean to reach this fortress. You are a fool to think so."

"My love is with Rama. I would sooner cast myself into the holy fire and die," Sita countered defiantly.

"Then you shall remain here as my captive! You have but two more months to give in to my wishes. Defy me further, and I shall be forced to end your life." With that, he stormed off in fury.

Through this tense exchange, Hanuman remained concealed, quietly observing from behind the trees. Remaining perfectly still, he waited for the right moment. He noticed that the *rakshasis* assigned to guard Sita began to nod off, one by one, and he finally found his chance to approach Sita.

Hanuman knelt respectfully at her feet as he chanted Rama's name softly. "Fear not, for I am Hanuman, Lord Rama's devoted servant and messenger. He has sent me to locate you. He longs for you and weeps for your return."

Sita regarded Hanuman with a mixture of curiosity and suspicion. "How can I trust your words? How do I know you are who you claim to be?"

She considered whether this creature before her could, in fact, be Ravana in disguise.

Hanuman reached into his pocket to show her Rama's ring. Handing it to her, he said, "This ring, dear Sita, is a token from Rama, sent to show you my true purpose, that I come in his name."

Hanuman, overjoyed at finding Sita, presents Rama's ring as proof of his identity.

The sight of this familiar ring reassured her, and she felt a surge of hope and relief. "This is indeed Rama's ring," she whispered, her voice shaking with happiness. Holding the ring tightly in her palm, she felt a renewed connection to Rama despite the vast distance that separated them.

Sita could not fight back the tears that streamed down her cheeks as she felt an extraordinary sense of life coursing through her, sensations that had long remained suppressed under the shadows of her captivity. "Oh, my child, you'd better tell me everything at once. How is my lord? And Lakshmana?" Her voice quivered with excitement from the fragment of strength and hope that had been returned to her with this unexpected and welcome news.

"Rama grieves for you every moment," Hanuman replied. He described Rama's tears for her and the depths of his sorrow, reassuring her once more that Rama was on his way to rescue her. "Keep faith; this separation will soon be over. Do not give in to sorrow, princess. He wishes you to be strong."

Their conversation, heartfelt and prolonged, brought comfort to Sita's heart. Hanuman, ever the dutiful messenger, then proposed to carry Sita back to Rama on his shoulders.

"I've endured this separation for too long," she replied, "and every additional moment feels unbearable. Like a bird, I wish to soar away at once back to my Rama, but I cannot bear the thought of returning to my own home in secrecy. I long for Rama to vanquish Ravana openly, avenge his cowardly act, and take me back to my home with honour."

Sita fixed her eyes upon Rama's ring. "Until I am once again united with my beloved Rama," she whispered, "I have this ring to cling to and save me from the pangs of longing and despair."

Sita, placing her trust in Hanuman, handed him her headdress as a token of her love and assurance of her well-being. "Please, take this to my lord. Give him every bit of my love and my heart."

The peace that had enveloped the garden was soon shattered as the *rakshsasi*, alerted to an intruder in their midst, raised an alarm. Other *rakshsasis* and *rakshasas* quickly joined them, swiftly encircling Hanuman, ready to attack.

"Who dares trespass here?" one *rakshasi* challenged, her eyes sizzling with fire.

But Hanuman, hardly to be deterred, swung into action. "Your mischief ends here!" he declared.

"You'll rue the day you crossed our path," another *rakshasa* threatened, growling with malice before he too was swiftly silenced by Hanuman's decisive strike. One by one, Hanuman subdued each demon that so much as dared approach him.

CHAPTER 26

Flames of Fury - The Capture of Hanuman and the Burning of Lanka

DETERMINED TO DELIVER A STERN MESSAGE TO RAVANA, HANUMAN set about creating a little avalanche of devastation in the Ashoka grove. This way, he would convey to Ravana the seriousness of his actions and warn him to leave Sita unharmed. He tore through the grove, uprooting trees and ravaging through the perfectly tended gardens. Climbing atop the temple, he proclaimed his allegiance to Rama, and predicted Lanka's imminent fall.

This act of rebellion, so brazen in its intent and spectacle, quickly caught the attention of Lanka's defenders, prompting the dispatch of an entire swarm of *rakshasa* warriors tasked with capturing the foolhardy intruder.

Even as he faced the massive *rakshasa* army, Hanuman pounded his chest with a resounding thump as his roar pierced the air, "Know that I alone can slay a thousand of you!"

The ground quaked under his forceful strides, and his roar - thunderous and commanding - reverberated throughout the grove. Hanuman met the advancing warriors head-on with spirited intent. He knocked down anyone bold enough to come near him, crushing them into dust with his overpowering might. His fearsome presence struck terror into the hearts of the *rakshasa* warriors, and soon, they were seen fleeing in disarray.

Finally, Hanuman allowed himself, wittingly so, to be captured by Indrajit, Ravana's eldest son. Hanuman was taken, as he had hoped, before Ravana.

In the grand court of Ravana's palace, Hanuman contemplated the tragic irony of Ravana's reign: a ruler who could have been one of history's greatest kings, doomed instead to be remembered only for his tyranny.

Steadying himself, Hanuman delivered a solemn message to Ravana. "An army of vanaras draws near your gates, and death is upon you, king of Lanka. Why make an enemy of Rama? By abducting the great Rama's wife, you have committed an unforgivable wrong. How did you ever hope to survive this? And did you think nothing of the well-being of your own people?"

He warned Ravana that he'd be met with unimaginable suffering if he did not return Sita safely and respectfully.

Ravana had heard of Hanuman's heroics at the Ashoka gardens and knew this was no ordinary monkey. Of course, he would never admit this openly. As Hanuman continued to deliver his warnings, Ravana's simmering rage boiled over. "Kill him," he commanded, his voice booming through the court like thunder.

Just then, Vibhishana intervened, "O great Ravana, forgive my interruption, but I must speak," he said, bowing respectfully. "Though this messenger's words may sting our pride, it would be wrong to put a king's envoy to death. That would violate the sacred rules of warfare that have guided our noble lineage for generations."

Reluctantly, Ravana settled on a different punishment - to humiliate Hanuman before all of Lanka. He ordered Hanuman to be paraded through the city streets with his tail set on fire. Among monkeys, the tail was a symbol of pride and honour, making this punishment especially degrading.

The *rakshasa* forces ushered Hanuman outside the hall to comply with Ravana's orders. They wrapped his tail with rags and ropes, soaking it in oil. As they did so, Hanuman displayed his powers by increasing his size and lengthening his tail. As he was paraded through Lanka's streets, large mobs gathered, taking delight in his apparent plight.

Hanuman would have sooner slain them than endure such humiliation, but he chose restraint, permitting them to set his tail on fire. Unbeknownst to the onlookers, Hanuman was shielded by Agni, the Fire God, and as a result, felt no pain. This parade presented Hanuman with an invaluable chance to survey the city's layout and defences, and gather crucial first-hand intelligence for the anticipated *vanara* assault.

At last, having completed his mission in Lanka, Hanuman shrank in size, effortlessly slipping from the ropes that had restrained him. This more diminutive form, he calculated, would allow him to move quickly and stealthily through Lanka to execute his plan while evading recapture. In a defiant parting gesture, he darted from rooftop to rooftop, his still-blazing tail setting parts of the city on fire. Panic and chaos gripped the *rakshasas* who ran in all directions. Before departing the city, Hanuman checked to see if Sita was safe and, having bid her farewell, doused his tail in the ocean before leaping into the sky. When he reunited with the *vanara* army, he regaled them with the tales of his exploits, which, so filled with mischief and daring, drew uproarious applause.

With his tail ablaze, Hanuman leaps across Lanka, engulfing large parts of the city in righteous flames.

Hanuman then swiftly made his way to Rama. No sooner had he touched down than Rama rushed to him in anticipation.

"I pray that you have news of Sita."

Hanuman held out Sita's headdress, and when Rama's fingers closed around it, something in his face came alive again. "With such great risk to yourself, you have helped me locate my beloved Sita. You have given me the will to live once more. I shall remain grateful to you forever for this gift of hope."

"I am your devoted servant," Hanuman replied, bowing his head to accept Rama's blessings.

Emboldened by the knowledge of Sita's whereabouts, the army began preparing for the long march to Lanka.

CHAPTER 27

Ravana Convenes His War Council

The account of Hanuman's ambush and sheer audacity sent tremors through Lanka. Hanuman's incursion was a breach of Lanka's formidable defences that directly defied Ravana's authority. Hanuman had not only located Sita within the island's confines but also finished off many of Ravana's most skilled warriors along the way. He then left a trail of destruction in his wake, setting portions of the city ablaze and compounding the insult. This succession of daring exploits had shattered the illusion of invincibility that Ravana had long nurtured.

When it was reported that Rama and a monkey army were about to invade Lanka and had reached the Mahendra Hills, Ravana convened his war council at once. His generals and advisors gathered in the grand chamber, their expressions grim, as they awaited his command.

"Let them come," Ravana boomed, "We will show them that the strength of Lanka is not just in its walls but in the unconquerable might of its king and his warriors. Ready our forces, fortify our defences, and let Hanuman's folly be the final daring of these insufferable fools."

The council erupted in agreement. With one voice, the council resolved to confront Rama and his forces in a battle to the death. In their eyes, Ravana was beyond mortal reckoning - a force so supreme that no enemy, human or divine, in all three worlds could dare to stand against him.

Time and time again, he had defied death, triumphed over gods and demons alike, and reigned undefeated through the ages. The council was determined to teach the young human prince and his alliance of *vanaras* a harsh lesson in humility.

Indrajit sneered at Hanuman's exploits. "Pay no mind to the monkey. His escape was nothing but a stroke of luck, and he is a low-life serving a beggar's cause. Had I not allowed his departure out of mercy, he would be dead by now."

"They are no better than lice, O Lord of the Rakshasas," the demons cried with malicious glee. "At the very least, this vast army of monkeys should make for a hearty feast." Cruel laughter echoed through the hall, growing even more boisterous when Ravana himself joined in their savage delight.

Ravana's war council erupts with declarations of absolute loyalty and calls for war.

CHAPTER 28

The Pleas for Reason - Vibhishana's Warnings Fall on Deaf Ears

AMIDST THE CLAMOUR FOR AN ALL-OUT WAR, ONE LONE VOICE ROSE in dissent.

Vibhishana, Ravana's brother, pleaded with Ravana to reconsider this dangerous course that would risk the destruction of the entire *rakshasa* race in a war that, he argued, was entirely avoidable. He pointed out the harsh truth that it was Ravana's own actions, the abduction of another man's wife, that had led to the present crisis.

"My brother Ravana," Vibhishana began, his voice steady and without artifice. "I will not resort to flattery or comforting falsehoods that please your ears. As you have surely noticed, I too have sensed the unease in our land and skies. By your actions, you have brought shame upon this great land of our ancestors. Lanka is under siege by peculiar omens brought forth by this wrongdoing. Strange howls from birds, animals, and beasts persist through the day, and even the nights cannot conceal the dangers that lurk. We must heed these omens. The only just and honourable course is to return Sita to Rama, with honour. You must then seek his forgiveness and allow for peace to be restored. To persist on this path of adharma is to court certain ruin for you and for all of Lanka."

Vibhishana's warnings were dismissed as overly guarded, even cowardly, by Ravana and his advisors.

Yet, another member of Ravana's family spoke up - Kumbhakarna, his giant brother. "Vibhishana speaks not without reason," he acknowledged, but bound by deep familial loyalty and swayed by the thrills of battle, he too would eventually capitulate to the sweeping calls for war.

"Though I do not condone the abduction of another's wife," Kumbhakarna confessed, torn between loyalty and conscience, "we are rakshasas, warriors by nature, destined for battle, and not given to yielding. I will stand by you to protect your honour as my brother and king. I shall unleash havoc in the skies for you. If it is your will, I shall slay Rama and drink his blood so that Sita may become your queen."

Indrajit, Ravana's son, also supported the council's combative position. He lashed out at Vibhishana and strongly opposed any mention of surrendering to the weak and inferior Rama.

Ravana, urged further by his sense of superiority, was determined to have the final word. "If I were to return Sita, I would become a laughing stock in the eyes of all gods and demons."

Despite the overwhelming opposition, Vibhishana continued to reason. "Rama is no ordinary mortal; he is none other than Vishnu himself. The battle that will be is not of armies but of wills and divine purpose. Some believe he came to Earth to put an end to your very evil."

"I fear Rama no more than I fear myself," Ravana roared in reply. "You lavish praise on him as if he were your own. Brother, your treacherous heart betrays a lack of true rakshasa valour and spirit. You, with your pretence of innocence and gentleness, are no more than a serpent and a coward, readily doing the enemy's bidding. Your place is not among us, and I shall not be sorry to see you go."

Vibhishana replied, knowing that Ravana's words had no true justification. "Your crown may gleam brighter than gold, yet its weight bends your soul toward darkness."

"I would sooner face a thousand deaths than surrender to those meek humans!" Ravana shouted over his brother's words. "Remember, perils attend the kind of righteousness you preach. It makes no more sense for you to stay in this kingdom than for me to hold you back. The time has come for us to part ways, brother."

Vibhishana still refused to abandon hope, holding onto the belief, however faint, that his words might yet penetrate the expanse of Ravana's delusion and avert the impending war and bloodshed. "Listen to me, my dear brother," he reasoned. "Your reckless pursuit of power is leading us all to damnation. At this rate, even Yama, the God of Death himself, will be unforgiving." But Vibhishana should have known better.

In response, Ravana banished Vibhishana from Lanka, branding him a traitor. He accused Vibhishana of wishing death upon him so that he could seize the throne of Lanka for himself.

"Take your cowardice with you," Ravana declared, "and never return, for there is no place in my kingdom for the timid and the disloyal. For your actions today, the world will forever remember you as a traitor."

With no hope of convincing his brother and finding himself isolated within the council, Vibhishana was forced to leave Lanka.

CHAPTER 29

Across the Mighty Ocean - Building a Bridge to Lanka

GRIEVING OVER HIS EXILE AND BRANDED A TRAITOR BY HIS BROTHER, Vibhishana made his way to Mahendra Hill.

With Ravana's words of humiliation still ringing behind him, Vibhishana used his magical powers to reach Mahendra Hill and sought an audience with Rama. Upon his arrival, the *vanara* soldiers, who generally distrusted every *rakshasa*, were suspicious of him. At first, they suspected it might be a set-up to mislead Rama, but after their initial hesitation, they opted to present Vibhishana to Rama.

In Rama's presence, Vibhishana detailed the events that transpired within the walls of Ravana's court. "You must believe me," he pleaded. "This, and only this, is my true state."

Rama, known for his ability to judge character, listened attentively to Vibhishana's words. Recognising the courage it would have taken for Vibhishana to defect from his own kin, Rama replied, "Vibhishana, you have acted with the care of a brother and the wisdom of a counsellor. You have forsaken the easy path of adharma and sought refuge in truth. I welcome you among us."

Rama's words and persona deeply moved Vibhishana, who in turn pledged his allegiance to him.

With their sights set on Lanka, Rama and his army advanced toward the ocean's shore. However, Rama soon realised that crossing the vast expanse was beyond anyone's capability, except for Hanuman. Seeking divine assistance, Rama devoted three days to prayer and fasting, appealing to Varuna, the Ocean God, for help. Yet, as the days passed without any response from Varuna, Rama's patience began to fray.

Rama stood at the ocean's edge and called out, "Hear me, Lord Varuna, I am Rama of the Ikshvaku Dynasty, son of the great king, Dasharatha. I have offered you my respect and prayers, yet you remain silent. Know this - I command weapons of unfathomable power, capable of drying up these pounding waves and turning this vast ocean into a barren desert. If you wish to avert such a fate, reveal to me the path to Lanka."

Rama drew his bowstring tight while preparing to release the devastating arrow, when suddenly its waters began to churn and swell. Recognising the gravity of Rama's forceful words, Varuna finally emerged and addressed him. "Rama, hero of the Raghu Dynasty, your bravery and righteousness are celebrated across the three worlds. Know that I too am subject to the unalterable laws of nature. Yet, within your ranks resides Nala, a masterful engineer and architect. He will build a bridge to take you across these waters. I will ensure the ocean stays calm during its construction and guarantee your forces safe passage during their crossing."

Thousands of *vanaras* were promptly enlisted to gather whatever they could find - logs, boulders, and rocks the size of fists. Even the tiny squirrels pitched in, contributing what their small bodies allowed. The construction of the bridge was a colossal endeavour by any measure. It started with laying sturdy wooden logs to form a solid foundation, upon which the large rocks were arranged meticulously for stability. The monkeys and squirrels diligently filled the crevices with smaller stones, gravel, and sand, levelling out and solidifying the surface, thereby reinforcing the bridge's strength. The bridge's construction spanned five days, symbolising the collective will and unity of Rama's army, who joined forces to achieve this remarkable feat of engineering.

The vanara army, with help from creatures great and small, builds a magnificent bridge to Lanka in their quest to rescue Sita

As night fell, Rama, Hanuman, and the *vanara* army made their way across the newly constructed bridge, abetted in their passage by the gentle waves and winds. As they approached Lanka, their chants of "Victory to Rama!" pulsated through the air as a powerful anthem of their quest for justice.

The army encircled the city, securing all possible entry and exit points in preparation for a siege. As they were laying the groundwork, they too couldn't help but take a moment to reflect on the city's stunning beauty - indeed, Lanka was a jewel of architectural wonder. Yet, even as Lanka's golden walls gleamed, greed and treachery festered like a wound within.

Still hoping to avoid the devastation of war, Rama made one final attempt to avert conflict. He chose Angada as his envoy, for the young prince's combination of youthful zeal and solemnity made him ideally suited to carry a final plea for peace to Ravana.

Angada entered the majestic city with a purposefulness that belied his youthful appearance. His directive was precise and clear: Ravana must immediately hand over the kingdom to Vibhishana, who cared more deeply for Lanka and its citizens. "Rama urges you to reflect on the well-being of your people and justice's sacred principles," Angada announced. "He believes Lanka can flourish in prosperity and fairness under Vibhishana's rule." He paused, letting his words settle, before adding: "This is not merely an ultimatum, Ravana, but a chance for redemption. Accept it, and you will spare both sides the inevitable horrors of war."

Seated on his ornate throne, Ravana listened angrily to Angada's message. The suggestion that he was unfit to rule his own kingdom and should abdicate his throne to a traitor struck directly at his pride and authority - words that, under normal circumstances, would have been unutterable. As Angada would soon discover, such words spoken against Ravana were punishable by death.

Flanked by his ministers and warriors, Ravana responded at first with a mix of ridicule and defiance. "Tell your king that Ravana, the Lord of Lanka, bows to no one - least of all an exile and his band of forest-dwelling outcasts. I will neither surrender my throne nor return Sita. If Rama wants her, let me see him try to take her by force."

But that was not to be all - Ravana was so furious that he ordered Angada's execution. Thankfully, the young *vanara* prince, quick-witted and agile, narrowly escaped. He returned to Rama's camp, his report marking the collapse of diplomacy and pointing to the grim inevitability of war.

CHAPTER 30

The Killing of Rama

SEEING RAMA'S IMPRESSIVE ARMY AT HIS FORTRESS GATES, RAVANA turned to a sorcerer named Mayakara. He tasked the sorcerer with breaking Sita's will by deceitfully announcing Rama's death. "She need only believe Rama is dead, and she will come around to me, surely," the demon king predicted.

The sorcerer displayed a bloodied head, crafted to look just like Rama's, as grim evidence of the lie.

And thus the ruse was set into motion as Ravana approached Sita with the bloodied head. "O Sita," he declared, "your Rama and the vanara army have been slaughtered, falling helpless before my mighty forces, which swept in under cover of darkness and killed them all - to the last man and vanara."

"Despair not," Ravana stated, "for I still offer you the chance to become my queen. Consider it well. Soon, I shall return for your answer."

Stricken with a paralysing terror, Sita felt her soul quiver. She drifted back and forth into consciousness, unable to tell if this was nothing but a sinister illusion cast before her or a horrifying truth.

In a whisper that bore the strain of her anguish, she murmured, "Though you have left me, my love, my heart shall hold you in death as it did in life.

Take me with you, for my existence without you is a fate more grievous than death." Saying this, she fainted again.

Among the *rakshasis*, one named Sarama, who had quietly grown fond of Sita, could no longer bear to see her in such a state. In an act of compassion, she leaned closer to Sita and whispered the truth in her ears. "Do not grieve, dear Sita," Sarama urged softly, ensuring no other *rakshasi* could hear. "Your beloved Rama and his brother are very much alive and will soon rescue you - they stand at the gates of Lanka, ready to unravel Ravana's deception."

Relief surged through her, and her heart leapt with joy at the thought of Rama and Lakshmana already at the fortress gates.

Meanwhile, oblivious to the failure of his ploy, Ravana oversaw his defences, confident in his fortress' security and the effectiveness of his sorcery. Yet, within the walls of his stronghold, the seeds of doubt and fear were beginning to take root among his own ranks - some began to question the integrity and strength of a ruler who placed his faith only in deceit and manipulation rather than in martial prowess and courage as befitting a true *rakshasa* warrior.

CHAPTER 31

Ravana's War Spies are Caught

WITH HIS DECEPTIONS EXPOSED, RAVANA ORDERED HIS FORCES TO assemble at the city gates and ready themselves for battle. For four tense days, an uneasy stillness hung over both armies as they stood at the ready, each in anticipation of the other's move.

During this uneasy lull, Ravana sent spies disguised as *vanaras* to infiltrate Rama's camps. Despite their cunning camouflage, the spies were quickly unmasked. Yet, rather than punish them, Rama allowed them to roam freely through the camp. "Go," he said, "and relay what you have witnessed here. Tell your demon king of this army's strength and fighting conviction. Let him know that we fight with dharma on our side. Let him also know that when pride blinds the mighty, their fall is all but inevitable."

The spies returned to Ravana with their observations, cautioning him against challenging Rama and reporting that his forces appeared disciplined, fearless, and battle-ready. Such accounts only served to inflame Ravana's temper. "You ignorant wretches," he thundered, "How dare you extol the enemy in my presence? How dare you recite praises of Rama before me? I am your king, while he is nothing but an exile! I will crush Rama and make Sita my queen! It is not I who am marked by Death, but he. It is not my days that are numbered, but his."

CHAPTER 32

Rama's Army Storms Lanka

AT THE BREAK OF DAWN ON THE FIFTH DAY, THE TENSION THAT HAD built up over the days of the standoff reached its crescendo. Both armies stood ready, their flags fluttering in the wind. The sound of conch shells and war drums would soon pack the air, marking the commencement of battle.

Standing tall before his assembled forces, Rama reminded them of the justice of their cause and the moral duty that called them to arms. "Remember why we fight," he called out. His gaze swept over the warriors before him - the *vanaras* who had left their homes, who had crossed oceans, and who had placed their faith in him. "This battle is not just for Sita's rescue," he declared. "Your dharma is to rise against the unrighteous, wherever and whenever they may tread."

He paused, allowing his remarks to sink in. "Today, we do not stand merely as warriors, but as custodians of truth and justice, fighting not just for ourselves, but for all who have known suffering under this tyrant's reign."

A clamour of assent erupted from the *vanaras*. Rama led his army, which made its way into the city with spirited cries. "Victory to Rama! Glory to Sita!"

The battle began. It was as ferocious as it was unforgiving.

The *rakshasas*, armoured in iron and gold, wielding swords, spears, and axes, had spent centuries fighting in disciplined formations, their tactics hardened through successive conquests through time.

But they weren't prepared for anything quite like this - the unorthodox, untamed fighting style of the *vanaras* caught them completely off guard.

The *vanaras* did not move like typical soldiers. They swarmed. They leapt. They fell upon their foes with primal ferocity. Their weapons were not forged in fire but were the raw, relentless forces of nature. Let loose, they were the unshackled spirit of the wild itself - brave and vehement.

Trees became clubs; rocks became projectiles; even teeth and claws became weapons of war against the sharpened blades, spears, axes, and bows of Ravana's forces. Lanka's streets witnessed massive loss of life on both sides with its stones soaked in blood. The *vanaras* appeared to be gaining ground and pushed Ravana's forces back as the demons struggled to hold position - but the question lingered: would their advantage last?

Rama and Lakshmana demolished many of Ravana's most seasoned warriors, including several of his sons. Ravana strode onto the battlefield in a fit of fury and desperation. He hurled the *Shakti* missile, a weapon of crippling power, at Lakshmana. The missile descended like a thunderbolt, striking Lakshmana's chest with immense force, knocking him straight away to the ground.

Seeing his fallen brother, Rama rushed forward and challenged Ravana directly. A furious fight erupted between the two commanding opponents. In the end, Ravana was grievously wounded, his chariot shattered, and his crown in ruins as he stood helpless before Rama.

Rather than delivering a fatal strike, however, Rama declared, "You fought bravely, yet now you stand incapable of continuing. Death looms over you, but I will spare you to fight another day. Depart now and recover. Return tomorrow when you are more worthy to face me."

This act of magnanimity, while offering relief, stung Ravana with shame. He hurriedly withdrew into Lanka.

Meanwhile, Lakshmana had regained his strength and returned to his feet. As the brothers stood side by side once more, Indrajit, Ravana's son, entered the fray. The two brothers fought on. With a barrage of powerful weapons, Indrajit struck down Rama and Lakshmana, leaving them unconscious on the battlefield. He then released deadly serpents upon the brothers that coiled tightly around their bodies.

Indrajit returned to Ravana and announced the presumed death of the two princes. "This war is in effect over," he exclaimed. "We have triumphed!"

Ravana was exultant and saw it as a proof of his side's superiority. "You have brought honour to our kind. It turns out that Rama and his brother were not as formidable as their reputation suggested. Good sense should finally prevail over Sita."

This turn of events cast gloom over the *vanara* ranks, causing them to fall back in disarray. In this moment of crisis, Vibhishana, always the voice of wisdom, moved closer. "Hold fast. The princes are not dead but have only sunk into a deep sleep."

As if on cue, Garuda, God of Eagles and *vahana* (mount) of Lord Vishnu, descended from the skies. Known as the sworn enemy of serpents, his coming sparked further hope among the *vanaras*.

Garuda, the mighty eagle and vehicle of Vishnu, descends to free Rama and Lakshmana from the deadly serpents that were let loose to bind them to certain death.

Anxious that the evil serpents binding themselves to the princes might crush them to death, Garuda swiftly chased each of them away.

Rama and Lakshmana awakened from their slumber, freed from what had seemed like certain death. Though dazed at first, they were soon restored to full strength and alertness, and ready to resume their place in battle.

News of this awakening got around like wildfire, erupting in celebrations among the *vanaras*. The jubilation eventually reached Ravana's ears, leaving him perplexed.

"Why do they rejoice when their commanders have fallen?"

His confusion turned to panic as the answer came swift and unsettling. "Sire, the princes are alive, full and well. They fight on with spirits undiminished. They move about the battlefield with the force of a thousand lions. Their army, too, is as firm as ever. This war, I daresay, is far from over."

As Ravana absorbed the grim reports of his generals' defeats and the unyielding spirit of Rama's forces, his willpower began to waver. In his palace, Ravana paced back and forth, deep in thought. The joy and cheers of the *vanaras* continued to gnaw at him. "How could they have survived? How can they continue to fight with such vigour?"

And as if the tides wouldn't stop turning against him, one after another, his finest generals - Vajradamshtra, Prahasta, and Akampana - fell to the strength of the *vanara* forces, compounding Ravana's dismay.

In truth, the war exacted an overwhelming toll on both sides. Each victory was dearly bought, as the *vanara* army also suffered shocking losses. The once resplendent Lanka turned into a horrific landscape steeped in a river of blood while raging fires painted the skies in shades of orange and black.

CHAPTER 33

Ravana's Desperate Gamble - Awakening a Sleeping Giant

RUNNING OUT OF OPTIONS, RAVANA TURNED TO HIS LAST HOPE TO revive the flagging spirits of his army - his brother, Kumbhakarna, a veritable force of nature and a giant amongst giants.

Ravana ordered a small battalion to awaken Kumbhakarna from his deep slumber, a state he had entered into after the meeting of the war council.

Kumbhakarna's sleep served as a mercy for humanity, for he feasted on humans daily, sowing terror in every direction. During his months of slumber, people enjoyed a brief escape from his terrible hunger. This strange cycle of destruction and relief resulted from divine intervention cleverly orchestrated by Saraswati, the Goddess of Learning and Wisdom.

Saraswati had thwarted Kumbhakarna's original wish during his boon from Lord Brahma. Instead of asking for the power of *nirdevatvam* (the ability to eradicate the gods), she cleverly manipulated him to ask for *nidravatvam* (incessant sleep). This way, Kumbhakarna's six-month-long slumbers became an unintentional shield for humanity.

Amidst the war's shifting tides, the demon king issues an urgent decree

to awaken Kumbhakarna, the mighty giant, from his prolonged slumber.

Rousing Kumbhakarna was no small feat; it was comparable to moving a mountain or stirring a dormant volcano. The task fell to hundreds of servants, who raised a deafening uproar with drums, conches, and the thunderous trampling of a thousand elephants around his enormous sleeping chamber.

When Kumbhakarna finally awoke to the pandemonium and beheld the mountains of food awaiting him, his reaction was one of mild amusement rather than true satisfaction. "This is diabolical, it does not do me much good; it barely tickles my stomach. Bring me more - much more," he bellowed, clearly underwhelmed by the gargantuan feast laid out before him.

The ministers, fully aware of the magnitude of their task, rushed to provide an even more impressive bounty of food, understanding all too well that Kumbhakarna's awakening was about more than just appeasing his appetite.

Once Kumbhakarna had eaten his fill, Ravana's senior ministers rushed in, their faces glum. The battle was turning against them. "The vanara army is fully upon us tearing through our forces," one minister warned. "Things look dire, my Lord," alerted another. "Our ranks are thinning rapidly. Even our most fearsome generals have fallen. Ravana himself very closely escaped death."

This news set off a burst of fury in Kumbhakarna. He was outraged at being left asleep while the kingdom's fate hung in the balance. Though every instinct pushed him to rush into battle immediately, he was persuaded to first seek a meeting with Ravana.

By now fully awake and briefed on the situation, Kumbhakarna's initial shock turned to reflection on the sequence of events that had led to the present crisis. Anger rose within him, and he appeared in no mood to hold back. "See, my brother, you have brought this upon yourself," he said bluntly. "You spurned Vibhishana's advice and dragged us headlong into ruin with your rash choices. And now look at the consequences."

Ravana, already strained by war's ongoing pressure, had little patience for Kumbhakarna's scathing swipes. He cut him off sharply. "Kumbhakarna, I did not have you awaken from your slumber so you could preach to your king. The time for such enlightenment is long past. Our kingdom teeters on the brink of ruin. What good is your strength if it cannot drive away the enemies from this great land of ours? Your unequalled strength is our last hope. Can I count on you to stand and fight for the honour and glory of your king and country?"

Ravana's fervent call for loyalty and the defence of his realm struck a chord with the giant. "My brother, my loyalty has never wavered," Kumbhakarna replied. "Be it in righteousness or folly, I stand at your command. I shall fight to my dying breath for you and our realm."

"Then move briskly, my dear Kumbhakarna," Ravana urged, "for time is not on our side."

Kumbhakarna was the embodiment of raw power. Impulsively emotional, he was always trying to prove his worth, especially to Ravana. With his chest thrust out and nostrils flaring, he lumbered onto the battlefield, wielding a mighty spear in one hand and a mace in another. The very sight of him sent spasms of fear through the *vanara* army.

The *vanaras* fought to check his advance, hurling massive rocks and uprooting trees in his path, but he swatted them aside as if they were mere pebbles. With every swing of his mace, he cleared swathes of enemies. His thirst for destruction was monstrous - not merely a warrior, he was a force of terror, feasting on his fallen foes as he advanced ahead through the battlefield. With each advance, he breathed new life into the *rakshasa* army, and for the first time, it seemed he alone could turn the tide of battle.

Even Rama, ever calm and unaffected, had to think quickly. He observed Kumbhakarna's movements, his sheer size, his relentless force - until suddenly, in the giant's seemingly perfect assault, he saw a weakness.

"Target his mobility," he commanded. "Lure him into the forest where his size - the very source of his power - will work against him. Move swiftly - strike and retreat before he can counter."

The *vanaras* followed Rama's lead, weaving through the trees, dodging Kumbhakarna's swings, striking from the shadows before vanishing again. This tactic was working, at least for some time, in causing some frustration to Kumbhakarna. But despite these manoeuvres, the tide of the battle indeed continued to tilt in favour of the *rakshasas*. Angada was knocked unconscious by a devastating blow; Hanuman himself was wounded. Sugriva was taken prisoner, and Lakshmana's weapons failed to slow the giant. Not even the severing of his limbs slowed his advance.

Morale among the *vanaras* crumbled, while the *rakshasas* rallied behind their unstoppable Kumbhakarna.

The battle had raged on, shifting like the tides, but now, it had come to a decisive moment when Rama called upon the *Indrastra*, a celestial weapon of unmatched accuracy, to be used only for the direst of situations. As Rama drew his bow, silence fell across the battlefield.

True to its mystical origin, the arrow streaked through the air like a piece of divine fire, until it found its target. In an instant, Kumbhakarna's head separated from his body and shot up to the sky like a blazing comet.

Horror gripped Ravana upon hearing the news of his brother's death. "My brother," he whispered in disbelief. "The unstoppable Kumbhakarna is no more," he mourned. "It feels as though I have lost my own limbs!"

In the cold quiet that followed, Ravana was forced to finally reckon with the true magnitude of his adversary. "The battle cannot be won by strength alone. Could Rama be more than a mere mortal?" he pondered, beginning to quiver with agitation. This soul-searching shook Ravana's bearings, filling him with sharp convulsions and forcing him to reevaluate his understanding of the war and the mystical forces arrayed against him.

CHAPTER 34

Hanuman Carries a Whole Mountain to Save Lakshmana

INDRAJIT, THE PRIDE OF THE RAKSHASA LINEAGE AND RAVANA'S SON, came forward to console his grieving father. "Do not lose heart, father," he said solemnly. "I will avenge my uncle's death."

This was no empty boast. Born as Meghanada, he had earned the title *Indrajit* (Conqueror of Indra) after his triumphant victory over Indra, the King of the Gods and Heavens.

"Rama and his allies must pay with their lives - every last one of them," Ravana commanded. "Promise me this, my son. Upon you rests the honour of our ancestors."

Indrajit stormed onto the battlefield. He let loose a merciless volley of poison-tipped arrows, each aimed with deadly accuracy at Rama and Lakshmana. "This marks your end," Indrajit proclaimed, seeking to avenge his family's honour and regain the battle's momentum. His assault was so rampant that it left Rama and Lakshmana weakened from an onslaught of wounds.

This time, Indrajit was determined to leave absolutely no room for failure. Having mastered dark magic, he planned to use it to destroy his enemy's will. Above the warfront he hovered with eyes full of destructive intent. With a simple hand gesture, he conjured a sight so actual and spine-chilling that it shocked even the most courageous *vanara* as they all staggered back in horror. Sita appeared before them, shackled and in distress. Indrajit, who then appeared beside her, grabbed her by the hair and killed her instantly before Rama and his soldiers could respond.

Rama fell to his knees in anguish. Indrajit successfully rattled the entire *vanara* army. The sight of the weapon, cruelly presented as the instrument of Sita's death, magnified their horror. The *vanara* warriors lost their fighting spirit after absorbing how deeply their leader was overcome by sorrow. The mighty Rama, whom they had followed into battle, had visibly fallen into despair before their eyes. Indrajit's laughter, malevolent and triumphant, deepened the demoralising effect of his illusion. Indrajit had played his hand well - and it had clearly produced the necessary impact.

Back at his palace, Ravana listened to the report of his son's triumph. Though briefly uplifted, Ravana remained cautious and on edge. This war had been anything but predictable. Rama's forces had repeatedly rallied and defied the odds. He turned to Indrajit and warned him: "Stay vigilant, my son. Do not make the mistake of thinking this battle is over. The enemy has proven their cunning and resourcefulness time and again. Do not underestimate them."

At the *vanara* camp, Vibhishana worked to bolster the spirits of the distraught warriors. "This is an illusion, nothing but a trick to weaken our will," he said, breaking through the despair. Vibhishana reasoned that Sita's death was simply a ploy to unsettle their morale. "Consider this: would Ravana, who has waged this entire war to claim Sita, truly allow her to be slain thus? Indrajit seeks to shatter us. But we must not fall for his deception."

Vibhishana's explanation brought comfort to Rama, and with it, the pall of despair that had settled over his forces began to lift. The *vanara* army stirred, gripping their weapons once more. Yet, no sooner had they regained hope than another blow fell. Lakshmana was found motionless on the battlefield, struck down by one of Indrajit's deadly weapons.

The sight of an injured Lakshmana produced currents of dread. Rama knelt by his brother's side, his hands shaking as he searched desperately for a breath, a flicker of movement, any sign of life at all. Overwhelmed by the possibility of losing Lakshmana, he whispered, "My dearest brother, how can I go on without you? You are my strength, my shield - my very heart. Do not leave me."

Tears welled in Rama's eyes as he pressed his forehead against Lakshmana's, his voice cracking. "If I have failed you, forgive me. If there is any justice in this world, may the heavens spare you."

With Lakshmana between life and death, the quest for locating the life-restoring sanjeevani herb becomes a desperate race against time.

Lakshmana teetered on the brink between life and death. The esteemed physician of the *vanara* army, Sushena, did everything possible to save him. Relying on his vast knowledge of ancient remedies and understanding of the body's workings, he applied all techniques available to him. Yet, despite his formidable skills, Lakshmana's condition remained fragile as he fought for each breath.

As a last frantic measure, Sushena called upon the legend of the *sanjeevani booti*, a mythical herb with remarkable healing powers. It was said to grow far across the sea in the Himalayas within the Dronagiri

Range's wild, remote expanses. The exact location of the herb was a mystery, and time was rapidly ebbing.

Recognising the urgency before him, Sushena turned to Hanuman, entrusting him with the mission of retrieving the *sanjeevani booti*. "You will not miss the mark," Sushena said, "for the truth will guide you."

When Hanuman reached the Dronagiri Mountains, he successfully identified the hill that had been described to him. However, he struggled to pinpoint the specific *sanjeevani booti* herb amidst the lush foliage. With precious moments slipping away and Lakshmana's life hanging by a thread, Hanuman made a bold decision - he uprooted the entire hill and, holding it aloft in one hand, soared into the sky.

The epic feat when Hanuman, unable to identify the specific herb, decides to carry the entire mountain that holds the cure for Lakshmana's life-threatening wounds.

As Hanuman touched down bearing the herb, Sushena wasted no time. He deftly identified the *sanjeevani booti* among the myriad of herbs. The physician prepared the remedy and administered it to Lakshmana with practised precision and haste.

Within moments of receiving the *sanjeevani booti*, Lakshmana's condition began to show astonishing improvement. His breath steadied, colour returned to his pale cheeks, and even his deepest wounds began to visibly heal. The *vanaras*, who had been holding their breath, let out a sigh of relief as Lakshmana's eyes fluttered open.

With Lakshmana restored to full health, Hanuman, ever dutiful, returned the uprooted hill to its rightful place in the Dronagiri Range. At a loss for words, Rama embraced the heroic and devoted Hanuman once he returned. "I am humbled by all you have done for me and this cause," he said at last. "Your friendship, so honest and faithful, has saved me over and over again."

As the battle resumed, Indrajit, frustrated by his repeated failures to best Rama, contemplated a forbidden path - a dark, sacrificial ritual meant to grant him invincible power.

Vibhishana forewarned Rama about this, who in turn tasked Lakshmana with preventing Indrajit from completing this dangerous ritual. Accompanied by Vibhishana and Hanuman, Lakshmana arrived at the site of the ritual just in time. A fierce battle of wills and warfare ensued. Lakshmana was able to break Indrajit's chariot, causing it to crash to the ground. The two warriors, evenly matched in skill and strength, continued their combat on foot, but neither could really gain the upper hand.

The course of battle shifted when Lakshmana, invoking a sacred *mantra*, drew upon the mighty *Anjalikastra*. He entered the requisite meditative trance, aimed and released this divine weapon, which finding its mark, sliced and severed Indrajit's head from his body. The *rakshasa* prince fell to the blood-soaked earth, his terror brought to a sudden and final end.

Upon learning of Lakshmana's victory, Rama was filled with joy and pride. "You have brought glory to the Ikshvaku race. Your valour will be celebrated and remembered for all of time."

CHAPTER 35

The Demon King's Last Stand

THE MOOD IN RAVANA'S CAMP HAD SHIFTED FROM SOMBRE TO CUTTING dismay. The reality that Indrajit, his son, the pride of his bloodline, who had once secured victory over Indra himself, had fallen decisively in battle was more than Ravana could bear. With Indrajit's death, Ravana felt lost and utterly alone. His anger compounded at the thought that his brother, Vibhishana, now fighting alongside his enemies, had a hand in this tragic outcome.

"My son, the mightiest of warriors, born of my blood, you who made even the King of Gods cower," he mourned. Ravana sank deep into the darkest enclosures of his mind at the sight of his fallen son.

Grim thoughts of retribution besieged Ravana. "The loss of my beloved sons, my beloved brothers - this is truly my darkest hour. What remains for me now?" After a moment of silence, his grief morphed into wrath as he visibly shook. "I shall kill Sita, for she is the root of all this misery."

With a soul shattered by grief, he justified his bitter resolution: "Since I do not have the assurance of her affections, there is nothing else left for me to do. Despite my endless declarations of love for her, she bears none for me in return. Yes, it is true; Sita lies at the heart of my burden and tragedy."

The *rakshasas*, roused by these visceral scenes, roared their allegiance and hailed their king. They bayed for Sita's blood - their cries of "Revenge! Revenge! Revenge!" spilt into a fevered chorus, echoing the raw and murderous emotions sweeping through every inch of Ravana's court.

The minister of the court, Suparsva, sought to temper the rising fury amid this hysterical atmosphere. He addressed Ravana, "O mighty Ravana, revered Lord of the Rakshasas, our King of Kings. Forgive me for speaking out of turn, but may I say that even in our sorrowful hearts, we must not descend to plotting a woman's death. Your extraordinary meditation, unmatched strength, and noblest stature elevate you above such departures from our ancestral ways. Acting on this impulse would bring shame upon the land that belongs to your ancestors. The sacred edicts left by those before us explicitly prohibit any acts of harm toward children or women. Let us instead focus our efforts on winning a decisive victory against our real enemies, Rama and Lakshmana."

Suparsva turned to the gathered commanders and rallied them with a clarion call to arms: "Let us hear the sweet proclamation that Rama and Lakshmana have met their end. For the cause and glory of our king, let us so resolve."

Ravana saw the wisdom in Suparsva's counsel and commanded his warriors back towards the real enemy. "Bring me Rama's head."

A newfound fervour animated the *rakshasa* ranks. They pressed hard against the *vanara* forces, dealing blows by the hundreds that seemed to alter the battle's momentum. But under the strategic command of Sugriva and Hanuman, the *vanara* army quickly regrouped and mounted a daring counterattack. Any fleeting advantage held by Ravana's forces rapidly disappeared.

The *vanaras* regained the upper hand and wiped out the *rakshasas*. The survivors fled into the forests to escape certain death. A pall of mourning descended upon Lanka, grieving the countless lives lost in a conflict rooted in Ravana's personal ego, which had brought them right to the edge of their forbearance.

CHAPTER 36

The Prince of Light versus the Lord of Darkness - The Final Battle

FACED WITH THE DIRE STATE OF HIS DWINDLING FORCES AND GROWING risk of defeat, Ravana's fury tightened its grip fully over him. He knew the time had come to face Rama himself and bring a finality to the battle once and for all. Wearing dark armour and drawing upon his deadliest weapons, Ravana mounted his majestic eight-horse chariot and thundered into the heat of the battlefield for a final showdown.

Squeals of anguish and cries of pain echoed throughout the kingdom, as strange omens shadowed the land. The once-blue sky had turned eerily dark.

Mounted on his majestic eight-horse chariot, Ravana enters the battlefield,

ready for the ultimate confrontation with Rama.

A hush fell over the battlefield as gods and mortals alike watched this epic contest between good and evil play out, between the Prince of Light and the Lord of Darkness. The entire cosmos held its breath in anticipation.

From the realms above, sacred forces rallied behind Rama. Indra, the King of Gods, understanding the righteousness of Rama's cause, sent his own chariot, steered by the masterful charioteer Matali, to assist the prince of Ayodhya.

The battle between Rama and Ravana escalated into a grand spectacle, a furious dance of weaponry under a sky fractured by the opposing forces of light and darkness. With a conjurer's command over the dark arts, Ravana manipulated his *astras* (weapons with mystical qualities) to cloak the day and night with malice, calling upon shadows and storms as manifestations of his rage. His many arms became deadly instruments of war and a spectacle of swift and terrifying artistry in the sky.

Yet, Rama, centred in an aura of tranquil might - born of deep spiritual practice, discipline, and sacred essence - countered each onslaught with the fidelity of a divine warrior. The battle soared into the skies, with both adversaries engaged in a breathtaking chase that circled the earth multiple times.

Sages had foretold this moment, and now, all of existence itself seemed to hold its breath. This epic clash cast a shadow over all creation, shrouding the sun with heavy clouds. As the hours passed, darkness and foreboding settled even deeper over the battlefield.

Despite all the wisdom he had gained from the ancient sages, Rama found this battle to be unlike any other he had faced. Ravana was an adversary without equal, wielding skills that defied the natural order of things. His mastery of forbidden knowledge allowed him to manipulate the elements at will - summoning violent storms to shroud the battlefield and conjuring impenetrable walls of fire to shield himself. Even as Rama's arrows struck true, severing Ravana's heads and limbs, they regenerated instantly, as if all the forces of nature conspired in his favour. Each moment of the battle was a clash not merely with Ravana but against the raw, primal power that seemed to bend, time after time, to the demon king's command.

Once more, Rama called upon the depths of his martial prowess, hallowed strength and spiritual fortitude. The clash of these titans, under the watchful eyes of the cosmos, was not merely a battle for dominion but a full unravelling of the eternal struggle between light and darkness.

CHAPTER 37

On Destiny's Edge - Rama is One Breath Away from Defeat

AS TIME DRAGGED ON, RAMA FELT SOMETHING INSIDE HIM START TO crack - his strength appeared to be giving way to the battle's ceaseless demands.

For the first time, he felt exhaustion starting to take hold. Seeking counsel, he approached a wise sage and shared openly this burden of mortal frailty. "My strength is waning. My body is worn, my spirit depleted."

The sage, a bearer of ancient wisdom, could perceive the full extent of the weariness in Rama's spirit. The sage placed a comforting hand on his shoulder and then spoke assuredly to him. "Turn to the Sun, Rama," he said. "It is the eternal source of strength. It is the fountainhead of life itself." Rama listened intently. "Invoke its blessing, and you will find the renewal you seek."

Rama knelt on the battlefield, lifting his gaze to the sky. Meanwhile, Ravana was summoning his next wave of dark weapons. With eyes closed and heart filled with prayer, Rama called for the Sun's life-giving grace.

The Sun's rays broke through the clouds, bathing him in their golden light. Through this sacred communion, a warmth spread through his body, steady and life-giving. Rama felt his spirit rekindled, his strength made whole again.

From the heavens above, the gods looked on with riveted attention as these events played out. Never before had the cosmos witnessed such formidable foes so equally matched in strength, skills, and intent.

Below, the remnants of both armies watched, hushed and spellbound. The clash before them was no longer just a war between two beings. It was a moment that would decide the fate of gods and mortals alike.

CHAPTER 38

At Long Last

UP TO THAT POINT, RAMA HAD TRIED EVERYTHING. EVERY WEAPON in his vast arsenal had been put to use. Yet, despite all his efforts, Ravana still stood, ferocious as ever.

Having come this far, the haunting spectre of failure loomed large over Rama. What if he failed? What if the demon who had so wantonly abducted Sita and caused so much suffering managed to escape justice? At stake were the anguish of their separation, the torment endured by his loved ones, and the countless innocents who had suffered under Ravana's rule.

Right then, Matali, his royal charioteer, leaned closer. "Rama," he whispered urgently, "my Lord, do you not remember what Sage Agastya once told you? He entrusted you with the secrets of the *Brahmāstra*, the weapon of the very last resort."

Indeed, the *Brahmāstra*, the most celestial of weapons, was never meant to be used lightly. In fact, it was intended more as a keeper of peace, to be used only if and when *all* other options had categorically failed.

As Matali advised, Rama realised the time to invoke the *Brahmāstra* was finally here.

Bearing upon his shoulders the burden of every soul that had suffered under Ravana's tyranny, Rama firmly gripped the *Brahmāstra*. He closed his eyes and began to chant. The sacred *mantras*, handed down through generations of sages, flowed through him like a river of divine power. Drawing upon the last of his strength, he entered a meditative spell, aligning himself with the blessed energy that was required to awaken this ultimate weapon.

The atmosphere around Rama electrified with the primordial power of ancient forces. With each invocation, the skies responded, pulsating with even more energy. A brilliant astral light surged across the battlefield, pushing back the darkness, illuminating the heavens with a preternatural glow.

Ravana grasped the shift immediately. He felt a great force forming around him and growing stronger by the second. The realisation struck him like lightning: if he allowed Rama to complete the ritual and invoke the *Brahmāstra*, death would surely follow. Desperate with urgency, he burst forward to attack, determined to shatter Rama's concentration.

But it was too late. The release of the *Brahmāstra* marked an Earth-shattering moment in the saga of gods and mortals - a weapon infused with the very essence of creation and the fiery intensity of a thousand suns. The Earth quaked, the sky split open to display a burning path, as the heavens themselves shook at the weapon's passage.

The warriors on both sides staggered while shielding their eyes as they stood humbled by the weapon's majesty. The winds ceased their furious howling to become utterly silent like death itself. Overcome by the sheer force of its divinity, those who remained on the battlefield - whether *vanara*, *rakshasa*, or human - bowed their heads and prostrated themselves in reverence.

The *Brahmāstra*, ablaze with celestial fire, struck Ravana's navel with unerring precision. This point on his body, imbued with his life force by a boon from Brahma, had made Ravana nearly invincible to the might of gods and demons alike. Yet this closely guarded secret, known only to sages and heavenly beings, was also his singular point of vulnerability - the target of Rama's final and fatal strike.

Ravana's body could not withstand the overwhelming shock. As his agony intensified, he crumpled under its impact. A deafening shriek was followed by a long mournful cry. The once-proud Ravana, his visage drained of colour, fell from his chariot. In stunned silence, the *rakshasas* watched their king fall lifeless to the ground.

The death of Ravana not only signified the end of a fearsome tyrant but marked a reaffirmation of the cosmic order - that no man, no demon, no god, however mighty, could escape the ordained balance of the universe.

A resounding chorus erupted from the crowd, their voices echoing the relief in every heart: "Long Live Rama!" "Long Live Sita!" "Long Live Lakshmana!" Even the gods, moved by the ups and downs of the battle, joined the celebrations. From the heavens, a cascade of flowers rained down upon Rama and his forces - a floral benediction of the likes never seen before.

With Ravana's final fall, the Earth grew steady once more. The winds shifted, their gentle caress dispersing the lingering dark clouds. The oceans heaved with gladness under the radiant light of the sun, while the trees swayed and rustled once again, whispering tales of peace, renewal, and life returning to its natural rhythm.

But amid the rejoicing, one figure stood apart from victory's glow. While the world celebrated, Vibhishana's sorrow carved a solemn contrast - a poignant reminder of the battle's personal toll. Kneeling beside his brother's lifeless body, he wept. "My worst fear has come true."

He looked at Ravana - the brother he had tried so desperately to save. "You, who once were immortal, now lie still. Why wouldn't you listen? Why couldn't you heed my warnings, my brother? What desire seized your heart so completely that you could not let it go?"

Ravana's queens assembled in grief, with Mandodari, his first and most cherished wife, leading their mourning. Despite his many flaws and the destruction he'd brought upon them all, Mandodari's love for Ravana remained undiminished. Now, amidst the ruins of what once was, she wept, "O my king, my heart. You, who once bested Indra, failed to see the bounds of your own ambition. I foresaw the futility of challenging Rama, an avatar of Vishnu himself. Yet, you, blinded by your pride, forged our doom."

Her sorrow, multiplied by the loss of her children alongside her spouse in a war birthed from folly, overwhelmed her. Overcome by grief, she collapsed amidst those gathered around her.

As the initial celebrations dimmed and the reality of the great battle's toll became apparent, Vibhishana approached Rama. Though Ravana's fate resulted from his own actions, Vibhishana remained determined to give his brother proper funeral rites. "My brother wrought much evil across the three worlds," he said to Rama, "but I must see to it that, in death, he finds peace. Will you allow me to conduct his final rites and give him an honourable funeral?"

Rama's response was infused with the same grace and wisdom that had characterised his command throughout this conflict - one that transcended the bitterness of war. "No one shall interfere with your brother's last sacred rites," he assured. "He fought bravely, and death takes away all hostilities and all wrongs. Do not grieve, Vibhishana, for his soul has now found liberation." With these words, Rama offered not just forgiveness, but a reminder of an eternal truth - that in death, all conflicts cease, and every soul is entitled to peace.

The sombre rituals that followed marked a fallen king's end. With Ravana's death, an era of war closed, and Lanka's new chapter began. Vibhishana's ascension to the throne was not merely a transfer of power - it symbolised a hopeful future for a land scarred by war and a future that promised healing, restoration, and peace.

CHAPTER 39

Rama and Sita are Reunited

WITH THE NEW KING'S BLESSING, VIBHISHANA'S WIFE, SARAMA - WHO had brought Sita comfort with her companionship and kind words during her captivity - was now appointed to guide her to freedom and reunite her with Rama. Sarama arranged for Sita to be received with the respect befitting her royal stature. Tears of joy welled in Sita's eyes, and this joy put strength into her weary limbs.

Sarama gently draped Sita in a *sari* (traditional draped garment) of exquisite beauty, its fabric shimmering like the first light of dawn. Jewels sparkled across her form, glistening with the promise of a new beginning. A beautiful red *bindi* (sacred scarlet spot) adorned her forehead. Sita's heart gushed with love. At last, the long, painful separation had come to an end. She could hardly contain her anticipation of reuniting with her dear, beloved Rama.

The instant Rama walked into the palace, Sita rushed toward him. She flung herself into his embrace, as if to bridge the distance that had kept them apart for what felt like an eternity. "Rama," she cried, melting into his arms as her love ripped through her, "My world - my everything."

Rama held her tightly, his eyes overflowing with tears and his heart brimming with joy too vast to contain. "Sita," he whispered tenderly, "no force in this world could ever keep me from you. You are my heart, my soul."

For that moment, it felt as if time itself stood still, as witness to the reunion of two hearts bound by unbreakable love. At long last, Rama and Sita were together again.

CHAPTER 40

Homecoming

As Lanka celebrated with the jubilations of victory and a newfound peace, an urgent celestial reminder soon triggered a shift of focus.

"Your odyssey endures, Rama," the gods decreed. "Bharata awaits your return, his heart heavy with the burden of days counted. You must hasten back to Kosala at once, for the morrow's light marks the final day of your fourteen-year exile, and upon it rests Bharata's solemn vow. He has sworn to immolate himself if you do not return by the appointed day."

To avert tragedy, Vibhishana, now the ruler of Lanka, harnessed the mystical resources at his command to summon the *Pushpaka Vimana*. This celestial chariot, famed for its beauty and swiftness, was summoned forth to ensure Rama's prompt return to Ayodhya, which would uphold the bonds of brotherhood and the sanctity of the promises made.

Outside Ayodhya's gates, a deepening shadow accompanied Bharata's vigil as fear mounted that Rama might never return. Preparing for the worst, he had even placed Shatrughana in readiness to take over his royal duties, ensuring that the kingdom's affairs would remain in steady hands.

Thankfully, events took a hopeful turn as Rama, Sita, Lakshmana, and their devoted companions Hanuman, Sugriva, and Vibhishana sped towards Ayodhya aboard the *Pushpaka Vimana*. The chariot, drawn by graceful swans, glided swiftly through the sky, retracing the path of their long journey. Below them unfolded the landmarks of their quest - the magnificent bridge to Lanka, the forests and rivers that both nourished and tested their endurance, and the kingdom of Kishkindha, where their fateful alliance with Hanuman was first forged.

At last, Rama and his entourage set foot on Ayodhya's soil. A great relief washed over Bharata. His brothers had returned, and with them, the rightful order to their world.

Bharata felt joyful as he approached the throne where Rama's sandals had rested all these years as an enduring symbol of his undiminished authority during his exile. He carefully lifted the sandals and placed them at Rama's feet. "My duty is complete, dear brother. These sandals, which have held your place, I return to you, the true sovereign of our land."

Rama, who was deeply moved by Bharata's devotion, commended him: "My noble Bharata, you are a true keeper of our legacy. Your actions have honoured our beloved father's memory and the highest ideals of our forefathers. May your innocence and truthfulness light our worlds forever."

Having fulfilled his promise to his father and performed his sacred duty, Rama then took his rightful place as King.

Silver clouds crowned the hilltops of Kosala, and the stately gates of Ayodhya, standing tall once more, rose towards the heavens in splendour. Homes across the land were cleaned and decorated. The kingdom was alight with the glow of *diyas* (traditional earthenware lamps) casting a warm, ethereal radiance over the land.

The entire kingdom was filled with ineffable joy, a fitting culmination to a tale that had tested the values of *dharma* and *satya* to their utmost limit. The people donned their most elegant dress as crowds of men, women, and children filled the streets to celebrate to the accompaniment of music and dance. They came forward to enshrine this triumph - of good over evil, justice over injustice, and *dharma* over *adharma*. Amidst the festivities, prayers rose to Goddess Lakshmi, invoking her blessings for prosperity and well-being for all.

Meanwhile, in the heavens, Lord Shiva turned to King Dasharatha with a gentle suggestion. "Go to Earth, great King, and see your sons once more." Grateful beyond words, King Dasharatha accepted without hesitation. King Dasharatha descended to Earth where he beheld his son Rama whose heart surged with happiness upon seeing his father again.

A storm of emotions brimmed within King Dasharatha, his eyes sharing his heart's affliction. "For many years, I have carried the burden of my wife's betrayal, but now I can finally lay my grief to rest. You, my son, are the greatest blessing that can be bestowed upon a father," he said, the warmth rising to his face, reflecting the depth of his realisation and relief.

Even the once-wicked Queen Kaikeyi found herself at a crossroads of redemption, her conscience stricken with regret. Once entangled by her own desires, the shadows of her past actions now lay bare before her. With a heart burdened with remorse, she sought Rama's absolution and forgiveness - a gesture that, by his acceptance, symbolised the healing of old wounds and the beginnings of new hope.

Under Rama's wise and just rule, the kingdom of Kosala entered a new age of glory, having never known greater happiness nor witnessed more enduring peace and prosperity.

Indeed, never before had the sun risen so beautifully over Kosala, nor had the lights from heaven shone as fully upon its walls. The breeze carried with it the promise of peace and abundance. Nature, in her grace, blessed the land with timely rains that nurtured crops, lush vegetation, and trees that bore the finest fruits anywhere on Earth. Squirrels scampered happily from branch to branch, birds flitted from tree to tree, golden blossoms dazzled in the forests, and millions of stars splashed across the clear night sky.

As the curtains fell on this epic saga, the Earth, now in better balance, finally witnessed the prevailing of good over evil, of virtue over immorality, of *satya* and *dharma* faithfully administered and upheld as both fundamental and necessary to the foundation of an ideal state - what we honour today as *Ram Rajya.*

The enthronement of Rama and Sita marked the return of harmony

and set the stage for the ideals of Ram Rajya to endure for times to come.

Appendices

FAMILY TREE

KING DASHARATHA

Wives:
Kaushalya, Sumithra, Kaikeyi

Sons:
Rama (son of Kaushalya)
Lakshmana and Shatrughna (sons of Sumithra)
Bharata (son of Kaikeyi)

Daughters-in-law:
Sita (married to Rama)
Urmila (married to Lakshmana)
Shrutakirti (married to Shatrughna)
Mandavi (married to Bharata)

Grandchildren:
Lava and Kush (Rama's children)
Angada and Chandraketu (Lakshmana's children)
Shatrughati and Subahu (Shatrughna's children)
Taksha and Pushkala (Bharata's children)

KING JANAKA

Wife:
Sunaina

Daughters:
Sita (adopted), Urmila

RAVANA

Uncles:
Maricha, Subahu

Sister:
Shurpanakha

Brothers:
Vibhishana, Kumbhakarna, Khara, Dushana

Wives:
Mandodari, Dhanyamalini, others

Sons:
Indrajit (eldest), Akshayakumara (youngest), Atikaya

SUGRIVA

Father:
Surya (The Sun)

Wife:
Ruma

Brother:
Vali

Nephew:
Angada (Vali's son)

HANUMAN

Fathers:
Vayu (The God of Wind), Kesari (adoptive, earthly father)

Mother:
Anjana

Son:
Makardhwaja (by some account born from a drop of Hanuman's sweat that fell into the ocean)

DIWALI

Diwali, commonly referred to as the Festival of Lights, is one of the most beloved and widely celebrated Hindu festivals not only in India but also across the world among people of many faiths. It shares similarities with the universal joy and warmth of Christmas festivities in the Christian tradition. Falling between mid-October and mid-November, Diwali heralds the end of the harvest season. It coincides with the *amavasya* (new moon), the darkest night in the Hindu calendar.

In the northern realms of India, Diwali commemorates the triumphant return of Rama, Sita, and Lakshmana from their fourteen-year exile in the forest after vanquishing the demon king Ravana. According to legend, the people of the kingdom lit diyas (traditional earthenware lamps) inside and outside their homes to illuminate the path for Rama, Sita, and Lakshmana, guiding them back home.

During Diwali, people light up their homes with oil lamps and candles to light up even the darkest corners, symbolising the victory of good over evil, and the conquest of light and knowledge over darkness and ignorance.

In the southern parts of India, the festival is tied to the legend of Lord Krishna's triumph over the *asura* king Narakasura, celebrating the liberation of captives from the demon's hold.

Across various regions, Diwali inspires a collective spirit of renewal and purity, prompting individuals to clean and decorate their homes, don new and colourful clothes, light *diyas*, and pray to Goddess Lakshmi, the deity symbolising wealth, prosperity and good fortune.

This pan-Indian festival brings together communities in a shared spirit of reverence and festivity highlighting the rich tapestry of India's deep cultural and spiritual heritage.

Since 2009, Diwali has been an annual celebration at the White House, a tradition initiated by former US President Barack Obama. This tradition underscores the festival's universal appeal and the shared human longing for unity, joy, and peace.

HINDU GODS

Unlike Abrahamic religions such as Christianity, Islam, and Judaism, which are monotheistic (belief in only one God), the Hindu religion is polytheistic (belief in many Gods).

At the heart of Hinduism is the concept of a divine trinity consisting of Brahma, Vishnu, and Shiva.

Brahma: Known as the Creator, Brahma is the divine force responsible for shaping and bringing not just the cosmic universe into existence but the endless cycle of creation that perpetuates the flow of life. He is the first member of the Hindu Trinity.

Vishnu: Known as the Preserver, Vishnu represents the sustaining force that upholds the universe's order and harmony. Through his various incarnations (*avatars*), including that of Rama and Krishna, Vishnu intervenes at critical junctures in history to restore balance and righteousness, embodying the eternal vigilance required to maintain cosmic equilibrium. He is the second member of the Hindu Trinity.

Shiva: Known as the Destroyer, Shiva oversees the dissolution of all that exists, for it is through destruction that renewal and regeneration are possible. Shiva's domain encompasses the cessation of existence and the promise of rebirth in a more perfected form. He is the third member of the Hindu Trinity.

Hindus believe in the cyclicality of life—everything in the universe is created, preserved, and then ultimately destroyed in order that it can be renewed in a more ideal form.

Aside from the principal deities, Hinduism celebrates an extensive pantheon of gods and goddesses, each with their distinct roles and attributes.

Ganesha: The offspring of Shiva and Parvati, Ganesha is distinguished by his elephant head. Revered as the remover of obstacles, he is also the patron deity of arts, sciences and wisdom.

Saraswati: The Goddess of Learning, Wisdom, and Music; wife of Brahma; her blessings are sought for academic success.

Lakshmi: The Goddess of Wealth, Fortune, and Prosperity, both material and spiritual. She is the wife of Vishnu. Sita (Rama's wife) is an incarnation of Lakshmi. She is often depicted holding a lotus flower.

Durga: A powerful and fearless goddess, Durga manifests divine feminine power and is worshipped for her strength and protective fierceness. Her duty is to restore *dharma*. She is known to be deeply loving and compassionate to her devotees while merciless to her opponents. She carries numerous weapons in her many hands, with which she destroys evil.

Indra: The King of Heavens, King of Gods, Indra embodies a warrior spirit at its most supreme. He is the protector and provider of rain, and also controls thunder.

Agni: The Fire God, Agni, holds a central role in Hindu sacrifices and rituals, signifying purity and transformation.

Surya: The Sun God, who is the source of life and energy, is often depicted riding a chariot drawn by seven magnificent white horses across the sky while illuminating the world.

Vishwakarma: The Divine Architect and Craftsman of the gods, Vishwakarma, is revered as the deity of creation and engineering.

Vayu: The God of Wind, Vayu, represents life force and breath, vital to the balance of the natural world.

Yama: The God of Death and the Underworld, Yama, oversees the afterlife and is responsible for maintaining justice by rewarding virtuous souls and punishing the wicked.

Hinduism's rich pantheon reflects the religion's profound and diverse understanding of the divine, allowing devotees to worship and seek blessings from deities that align with their spiritual needs and aspirations. These deities, each with distinct roles and attributes, represent the cosmic forces that govern creation, preservation, and transformation, as well as the virtues and values central to human life.

EPICS

MAHABHARATA

The Mahabharata, one of India's two epic poems alongside *The Ramayana*, ranks among the world's most important works in world literature, along with the Bible and Quran. It was composed by Sage Vyasa during the 4th century BCE and stands as the longest poem ever written, comprising approximately 1.8 million words. In a remarkable fusion of the divine and temporal, the legend holds that Sage Vyasa dictated the verses to Lord Ganesha, who transcribed them.

The epic narrates the story of the intense rivalry between two families of cousins, the Pandavas (the five noble sons of King Pandu) and the Kauravas (the one hundred sons of the blind King Dhritarashtra), as they vie for control of the throne of Hastinapur.

Dhritarashtra, the elder of the two princes of Hastinapur, was the rightful heir to the throne. But fate had other plans. Because he was blind, the crown passed instead to his younger brother, Pandu. Pandu would prove to be a formidable ruler. Under his reign, the kingdom flourished, its borders expanded through conquest, and its people thrived. But victory and power were never his true pursuits. Content with all he had built, Pandu chose to step away from the burdens of rule. Seeking peace and reflection, he retreated to the forest with his wives, Kunti and Madri. Before leaving, he entrusted the kingdom to Dhritarashtra, placing its fate in his brother's hands.

As time passed, Yudhishthira, the son of the then-deceased King Pandu, was declared heir apparent. However, this angered Dhritarashtra's eldest son, Duryodhana. As the narrative unfolded, Duryodhana manipulated events, leading to a fateful game of dice in which the Pandavas lost. This loss was used to banish them to the forest in exile for twelve years while also stipulating that they remain incognito for the thirteenth year.

King Pandu's children (Yudhishthira, Bhima, Arjuna, and the twins Nakula and Sahadeva) were forced out of Hastinapur and sent to a dangerous and desolate forest.

Upon the Pandavas' return at the end of their exile, Duryodhana refused to cede control of Indraprastha as promised. This refusal set the stage for the Great Battle of Kurukshetra, a harrowing eighteen-day battle in which all the Kauravas perished and the Pandavas, with Lord Krishna on their side, emerged victorious, albeit at a staggering human cost. Yudhishthira was then crowned King of Hastinapur and Indraprastha, which he ruled for thirty-six glorious years.

The Pandavas exemplified the pursuit of the *purusharthas* (goals of life), which are *dharma* (duty), *artha* (wealth), *kama* (pleasure), and *moksha* (liberation) as the pillars of a complete and fulfilling life.

In the end, all the characters found their way to heaven and were eventually reunited with their cousins.

THE ILIAD AND THE ODYSSEY

Only a handful of epics describe events of such monumental importance that they have an everlasting impact on the culture and society from which they originate. *The Iliad* and *The Odyssey* are two such poems of Greek origin. These Greek epics, foundational to Western literary tradition, explore heroism, honour, and the ethical dilemmas of human existence.

Homer is credited with composing both *The Iliad* and *The Odyssey*.

Written in the mid-8th century BCE, The Iliad is set during the Trojan War, which was a long siege of the city of Troy by opposing Greek factions, and centres on the never-ending battle between King Agamemnon and Achilles, the world's most formidable warrior at the time. The narrative arc chronicles the intense final week of the Trojan War - underscored by personal vendettas, divine interventions, and the tragic futility of war.

Achilles leads the Myrmidons against the Trojans. Helen of Troy, the most beautiful woman in the world, is wed to King Menelaus. She becomes the emblem of the war's genesis as her elopement with Paris of Troy ignites a conflict that would span generations.

The Odyssey, serving as *The Iliad*'s narrative successor, charts the protracted homeward odyssey of Odysseus, King of Ithaca, in the aftermath of Troy's fall. What should have been a month-long journey lasts a full ten years. Renowned for his intelligence, Odysseus is the one who devises the iconic Trojan Horse strategy to infiltrate Troy and secure victory.

Odysseus' journey home stretched ten long years beyond the war's end, marked by divine whims, mythical beasts, and relentless trials of his wit and endurance. Upon Odysseus' return to Ithaca, he discovered that his kingdom had descended into chaos. Suitors besieged his estate and took control of his home because they believed Odysseus had died and wanted to marry Penelope. But Odysseus was no ordinary man. By applying his intelligence, bravery, and determination he won back his position while bringing his family and household back under control and reestablishing his rule.

While *The Ramayana* and *The Mahabharata* centralise *dharma* - duties, virtues, and the moral law - as the guiding principle of life and conduct, the Greek epics of Homer exalt the pursuit of *kleos*, which is about attaining glory through great deeds. This dichotomy reflects the cultural variances in the conception of heroism and the human condition. In the Greek ethos, personal valour and the legacy of one's deeds underscore a hero's worth. In contrast, the Indian epics advocate for righteousness, adherence to duty, and the cosmic order as the essence of true heroism, reflecting a worldview that values collective welfare and moral integrity over personal glory.

Despite these thematic divergences, both the Greek and Indian epics traverse the universal themes of justice, loyalty, sacrifice, and the human experience marked by a perennial struggle against adversity. By transcending their cultural origins, they highlight humanity's unceasing quest for fundamental meaning amidst the twists of fate, and the search for one's place within our vast existence.

GLOSSARY (HINDI)

1. **asura (असुर)**: In Hindu mythology, *asuras* are powerful beings often portrayed as antagonists of the *devas* (gods). While they are commonly associated with darkness and chaos, their nature is far more complex than simply being "evil." In early Vedic texts, *asuras* were not inherently malevolent - they were divine entities, much like the *devas*, with their own strengths and ambitions. Over time, however, the term took on a more adversarial meaning, with *asuras* coming to represent forces that challenge the cosmic order. This evolving portrayal is central to epics like *The Ramayana* and *The Mahabbharata*, where *asuras* stand in opposition to the *devas*, not merely as villains but as forces that test the boundaries of righteousness. The term highlights the nuanced dynamics of good versus evil within Hindu cosmology, emphasising the ongoing struggle between these celestial beings. Their presence underscores the deeper philosophical idea that good and evil are not always absolute but part of an ongoing struggle that shapes the universe.

2. **bindi (बिंदी)**: Traditionally a red dot worn on the forehead between the eyebrows, the *bindi* symbolises the third eye in Hinduism. While it is primarily associated with married Hindu women, it's also worn by men and unmarried women for religious purposes. The *bindi* is thought to retain energy and strengthen concentration, and its position represents the *Ajna Chakra* or the seat of concealed wisdom. Over time, the *bindi* has also evolved into a fashion statement available in various colours and designs.

3. **brahmāstra (ब्रह्मास्त्र)**: *The Brahmāstra* is one of the most destructive and powerful supernatural weapons in Hindu mythology. Created by Brahma, it is said to contain the energy and power of the universe's creation. Invoked through specific *mantras*, it is represented as a fiery missile that, once launched, cannot be withdrawn. Its use has devastating effects, comparable to a modern-day nuclear weapon in its destructiveness. *The Brahmāstra* is traditionally considered a weapon of last resort, used only in the direst circumstances due to its potential to cause mass destruction and irreversible environmental impact. It was only available to those who had the required knowledge and spiritual prowess. The possession and use of such a weapon are closely tied to the practitioner's mastery of specific divine incantations and their moral and spiritual merit.

4. **brahmanic (ब्राह्मणिक)**: pertaining to the ancient form of Hinduism focused on the rituals and philosophies described in *Vedas* and *Brahmanas*. This period marked a transition from the Vedic sacrificial rituals to more symbolic and philosophical interpretations of those texts. The term is often associated with the priestly class (Brahmins) who perform these rituals and maintain the sacred knowledge.

5. **dharma (धर्म)**: a complex and multifaceted concept in Hinduism, *dharma* represents duty, righteousness, law, and moral order. It is considered the very foundation that upholds the universe and society. Each individual's *dharma* varies depending on their stage in life, caste, and specific circumstances. Upholding one's *dharma* is believed to contribute to the order and functioning of the cosmos.

6. **Ganesha (गणेश)**: the elephant-headed god, Ganesha, is one of the most cherished deities in Hinduism. Known as the remover of obstacles and the God of Beginnings, he is often invoked at the start of any new venture or journey. According to mythology,

Ganesha was created by Parvati and given life by Shiva's glance. His elephant head symbolises wisdom, understanding, and a discerning intellect that one must possess to attain perfection in life.

7. **kartik (कार्तिक)**: this is the eighth month in the Hindu lunar calendar, following *Ashwin* and preceding *Margashirsha*, corresponding roughly to October-November in the Gregorian calendar. This month is part of a sequence of months: *Chaitra, Vaishakha, Jyeshtha, Ashadha, Shravana, Bhadrapada, Ashwin, Kartik, Margashirsha, Pausha, Magha, and Phalguna*. This sacred month is marked by significant festivals like *Diwali* and *Bhai Dooj* that celebrate the triumph of light over darkness and sibling bonds respectively. Devotees engage in rituals such as *Kartik Snan*, dawn baths in holy rivers, which are believed to purify the soul. This period is crucial for the worship of deities like Lord Vishnu and Shiva, embodying a time of spiritual reflection and renewal.

8. **kshatriya (क्षत्रिय)**: this term refers to the warrior and ruler class in the traditional Hindu Varna system. They were responsible for protecting society by fighting in wars and governing land. The *Kshatriyas* were considered the upholders of *dharma* and were expected to be brave, noble, and just in their actions. Historically, many famous Indian kings and warriors, including Arjuna and Rama, were *Kshatriyas*.

9. **Lakshmi (लक्ष्मी)**: The Hindu goddess of wealth, fortune, power, luxury, beauty, fertility, and auspiciousness. She is the wife of Vishnu and plays a crucial role in the maintenance of the world's wealth and resources. During *Diwali*, the festival of lights, Hindus offer prayers to Lakshmi to invite prosperity and wealth into their homes. She is often depicted holding a lotus, a symbol of beauty, purity, and fertility.

10. **mantra (मंत्र)**: a *mantra* is a sacred utterance, syllable, word, or group of words in Sanskrit believed to have psychological and spiritual powers. Typically recited during Hindu prayers and meditative practices, *mantras* are considered to carry divine vibrations which, when articulated with devotion and precision, can produce transformative effects. Popular examples include the *Gayatri Mantra*, which is chanted for enlightenment, and the *Maha Mrityunjaya Mantra*, used for healing and invoking divine protection. *Mantras* help focus the mind, achieve deeper states of awareness, and connect the practitioner to the divine.

11. **moksha (मोक्ष)**: in Hinduism, *moksha* is the ultimate goal of human existence. It represents liberation from the cycle of birth and rebirth (*samsara*) and the end of all worldly suffering. Achieving *moksha* involves realising one's true nature as *atman* (soul) and its unity with *Brahman*, the ultimate reality. This liberation is often associated with spiritual enlightenment and detachment from material desires.

12. **rakshasas (राक्षस)**: mythological beings often portrayed as demons in Hindu texts, *rakshasas* are known for their powerful and malevolent natures, often opposing the gods and creating chaos in the world. They are sometimes also depicted as more nuanced characters with their own codes of honour and morality. For example, Vibhishana from *The Ramayana* was a *rakshasa*, but was righteous and sided with Rama against his brother Ravana.

13. **satya (सत्य)**: *Satya* (truth) is a fundamental concept in Hindu philosophy. It refers to being truthful in one's thought, speech, and action. It is considered essential for moral and spiritual growth. The concept extends beyond mere factual accuracy to encompass living a life that is in harmony with the universal truth, which includes ethical and virtuous behaviour.

14. **Surya (सूर्य)**: the sun god in Hindu mythology, Surya is revered as the source of life and energy. He is often depicted riding a chariot drawn by seven horses, representing the seven colours of sunlight or the seven days of the week. Surya is worshipped daily in many Hindu households, and special prayers are offered to him in the morning. He is considered the eye of the universe, the soul of all that moves and is stationary.

15. **tapasya (तपस्या)**: this term refers to spiritual practices of austerity and discipline. *Tapasya* is undertaken to purify the body and mind, attain spiritual power, and achieve closer communion with the divine. It often involves rigorous practices like fasting, meditation, and abstinence from physical pleasures. In Hindu epics, many characters perform *tapasya* to gain boons from the gods.

16. **triloka (त्रिलोक)**: in Hindu cosmology, *Triloka* refers to the concept of three worlds or realms: *Swarga* (heaven), *Prithvi* (earth), and *Patala* (underworld). These realms are inhabited by gods, humans, and demons respectively. The concept illustrates the layered structure of the universe and the interconnectedness of different realms of existence.

17. **vedas (वेद)**: these ancient Indian scriptures form the foundation of Hindu religious and philosophical thought. Comprising four main texts - *Rigveda*, *Yajurveda*, *Samaveda,* and *Atharvaveda* - the *Vedas* contain hymns, rituals, prayers, and spiritual teachings. They are considered divine revelations heard by ancient sages and were transmitted orally before being written down.

18. **yagna (यज्ञ)**: a sacred Hindu ritual involving offerings made to the gods, typically through fire. *Yagna* is performed to maintain cosmic order and harmony, seek divine favour, and ensure prosperity and well-being. It often involves chanting of *Vedic* mantras, offering of *ghee* (clarified butter), grains, and other sacred substances into a

consecrated fire. The ritual underscores the importance of sacrifice and giving in Hindu philosophy.

19. **yuga (युग)**: in Hindu cosmology, a *yuga* refers to a cosmic age, marking different phases in the moral and spiritual evolution of the world. There are four *yugas* in a repeating cycle:

    - *Satya Yuga* - The Golden Age, an era of truth, righteousness, and purity
    - *Treta Yuga* - The decline begins; virtue remains but is no longer absolute
    - *Dvapara Yuga* - Morality weakens further, conflicts increase, and spiritual wisdom fades
    - *Kali Yuga* - The present age, marked by chaos, corruption, and spiritual decline

Each *yuga* is believed to shape human civilisation, reflecting the rise and fall of righteousness over time. According to Hindu texts, at the end of *Kali Yuga*, the cycle will reset, bringing a new *Satya Yuga* and restoring balance to the world.

GLOSSARY (ENGLISH)

1. **abet** (verb); uh-BET: to help or encourage someone to do something wrong or illegal

   synonyms: assist, support, aid, encourage, provoke

2. **abominable** (adjective); uh-BOM-uh-nuh-buhl: extremely unpleasant or disgusting, often in a way that causes moral revulsion

   synonyms: detestable, loathsome, repulsive, revolting, vile

3. **absolution** (noun); ab-suh-LOO-shun: formal release from guilt or blame from having done something wrong

   synonyms: forgiveness, pardon, mercy, freeing from blame, grace

4. **adversary** (noun); AD-ver-ser-ee: one's opponent or competitor in a contest, conflict, or dispute

   synonyms: enemy, opponent, antagonist, foe, competitor

5. **allegiance** (noun); uh-LEE-juhnss: loyalty or commitment to a superior or to a group or cause

   synonyms: loyalty, fidelity, faithfulness, obedience, devotion

6. **annihilate** (verb); uh-NYE-uh-layt: to destroy completely; obliterate

   synonyms: destroy, demolish, wipe out, obliterate, eliminate

7. **apathy** (noun); AP-uh-thee: a state of indifference or lack of enthusiasm, interest, or concern about a situation or event *synonyms:* indifference, disinterest, unresponsiveness, lethargy, detachment

8. **appeasing** (verb); uh-PEEZ-ing: trying to make someone calm or less hostile by agreeing to their demands

   synonyms: calming, pacifying, soothing, mollifying

9. **artifice** (noun); AHR-tuh-fis: clever or cunning trick used to deceive others

   synonyms: cunning, trickery, deceit, duplicity, guile

10. **atonement** (noun); uh-TONE-ment: the act of making amends for a wrong or sin

    synonyms: reparation, redemption, compensation, restitution, penance

11. **audacious** (adjective); aw-DAY-shus: displaying daring confidence and a readiness to take bold or unexpected risks

    synonyms: bold, daring, fearless, intrepid, brave

12. **austerity** (noun); aw-STER-i-tee: a stern and serious quality; a simple, plain, and disciplined way of living without luxury or excess

    synonyms: severity, strictness, frugality, simplicity, restraint

13. **besotted** (adjective); bih-SOT-id: deeply infatuated or completely in love, often to the point of foolishness

    synonyms: infatuated, charmed, smitten, captivated, obsessed

14. **blatant** (adjective); BLAYT-unt: done openly and unashamedly without worrying what others think

    synonyms: shameless, glaring, obvious, undisguised, clear

15. **boisterous** (adjective); BOY-ster-uhs: noisy, energetic, and cheerful in a rowdy or unrestrained way
synonyms: rowdy, exuberant, lively, rambunctious, spirited

16. **capitulate** (verb); kuh-PICH-uh-leyt: to stop fighting an enemy or opponent and agree to their demands; surrender
synonyms: surrender, yield, give in, submit, concede

17. **categorically** (adverb); kat-uh-GOR-i-kuh-lee: in a very clear and definite way, without any doubt or conditions
synonyms: definitely, clearly, unambiguously, absolutely, firmly

18. **celestial** (adjective); suh-LES-chul: positioned in or relating to the sky, or outer space; celestial bodies refer to the sun, moon, and stars
synonyms: heavenly, astronomical, extraterrestrial, stellar, cosmic

19. **chide** (verb); CHYD: to scold or rebuke gently
synonyms: reprimand, reproach, scold, rebuke, admonish

20. **colossal** (adjective); kuh-LOS-ul: extremely large or great
synonyms: enormous, gigantic, huge, massive, immense

21. **communion** (noun); kuh-MYOON-yuhn: a deep emotional or spiritual connection with someone or something
synonyms: connection, closeness, intimacy, unity, sharing

22. **conciliatory** (adjective); kuhn-SIL-ee-uh-tor-ee: intended to calm, pacify, or make peace, especially after a conflict
synonyms: appeasing, peacemaking, soothing, pacifying, compromising

23. **condone** (verb); kuhn-DOHN: accept and allow (wrong or harmful behaviour) to continue
synonyms: overlook, allow, let pass, ignore

24. **confidant** (noun); KON-fi-dant: a person with whom one shares private matters or secrets in trust

synonyms: trusted friend, adviser, companion, counsellor

25. **conjure** (verb); KUHN-jur: make something appear unexpectedly or seemingly from nowhere as if by magic

synonyms: summon, produce, create, generate

26. **conscience** (noun); KON-shuhns: an internal sense of morality that helps distinguish between right and wrong actions

synonyms: moral sense, scruples, ethics, morality, principles

27. **contrive** (verb); kuhn-TRYV: create or bring about by deliberate use of skill

synonyms: devise, plan, concoct, fabricate, invent

28. **countenance** (noun); KOWN-tuh-nuhns: a person's facial expression or appearance, especially as an indication of mood or character

synonyms: face, expression, appearance, look, demeanour

29. **crescendo** (noun); kruh-SHEN-doh: a gradual increase in loudness or intensity, especially in music or emotion

synonyms: build-up, escalation, surge, rise, climax

30. **debris** (noun); DEB-ree: the scattered pieces left over after something has been destroyed or broken

synonyms: rubble, wreckage, fragments, remains, ruins

31. **delirious** (adjective); duh-LEER-ee-us: in a state of extreme excitement or happiness that can cause confusion or make someone act crazy; also used to describe being very confused or disoriented because of illness

synonyms: excited, thrilled, wild, confused, muddled

32. **depleted** (adjective); dih-PLEE-tid: used up or worn out, especially in terms of energy or resources
synonyms: drained, exhausted, spent, empty, reduced

33. **destiny** (noun); DES-tuh-nee: a predetermined path or series of events that shapes a person's future
synonyms: fate, fortune, lot, providence, preordination

34. **diabolical** (adjective); dye-uh-BAW-li-kuhl: extremely evil or wicked, often in a clever or cruel way
synonyms: fiendish, demonic, wicked, malevolent, sinister

35. **diminutive** (adjective); dih-MIN-yuh-tiv: extremely or unusually small
synonyms: tiny, small, mini, petite, minute

36. **distraught** (adjective); dis-TRAWT: deeply upset and agitated, often due to worry or grief
synonyms: distressed, troubled, frantic, heartbroken, devastated

37. **ego** (noun); EE-goh: a person's sense of self-esteem or self-importance
synonyms: self-image, pride, self-worth, identity, self regard

38. **embody** (verb); em-BOD-ee: to represent a quality or idea perfectly
synonyms: personify, exemplify, represent, incarnate, manifest

39. **eminent** (adjective); EM-uh-nent: (of a person) famous and respected within a particular sphere or profession
synonyms: distinguished, renowned, illustrious, prestigious, prominent

40. **encompassing** (adjective); en-KUM-puh-sing: surrounding or holding within; including everything
synonyms: complete, comprehensive, extensive, all-embracing, all-inclusive

41. **ensnare** (verb); en-SNAIR: to trap or catch someone or something so they can't escape
synonyms: trap, entangle, capture, lure, hook

42. **enthralling** (adjective); en-THRAW-ling: capturing and holding one's full attention
synonyms: captivating, mesmerising, riveting, entrancing, fascinating

43. **estrange** (verb); e-STRAYNJ: to cause (someone) to no longer be close, friendly, or affectionate with someone
synonyms: alienate, distance, drive apart, separate, disaffect

44. **ethereal** (adjective); ih-THEER-ee-uhl: extremely delicate and beautiful in a way that seems not of this world
synonyms: delicate, exquisite, spiritual, elegant, graceful

45. **ethical** (adjective); ETH-i-kuhl: relating to moral principles and beliefs that help decide what is right and wrong
synonyms: moral, principled, virtuous, righteous, right-minded

46. **extol** (verb); ex-TOL: to praise somebody or something very much
synonyms: praise, laud, acclaim, exalt, eulogise

47. **exultant** (adjective); eg-ZUL-tant: feeling extremely proud or happy
synonyms: jubilant, triumphant, joyful, elated, ecstatic

48. **fealty** (noun); FEE-uhl-tee: a promise of loyalty and support, usually to a leader, country or cause
synonyms: loyalty, devotion, allegiance, faithfulness, commitment

49. **feeble** (adjective); FEE-buhl: lacking strength, especially due to age or illness
synonyms: weak, frail, delicate, powerless, infirm

50. **feign** (verb); FAYN: pretend to be affected by a feeling, state, or injury; to make to look as if it's true or genuine when it isn't
synonyms: simulate, fake, sham, affect, pretend

51. **fellowship** (noun); FEL-oh-ship: a feeling of friendship, especially between people who have common interests
synonyms: camaraderie, companionship, company, society, community

52. **fervent** (adjective); FUR-vuhnt: showing very strong and sincere feelings, especially enthusiasm or belief
synonyms: passionate, intense, eager, devoted, wholehearted

53. **fidelity** (noun); fih-DEL-i-tee: faithfulness to a person, cause, or belief, shown through loyalty or support
synonyms: loyalty, faithfulness, devotion, allegiance, constancy

54. **fiendish** (adjective); FEEN-dish: extremely cruel or wicked, resembling or characteristic of a demon or evil spirit
synonyms: evil, diabolical, wicked, devilish, unpleasant

55. **fleeting** (adjective); FLEET-ing: existing or lasting for a brief moment before disappearing
synonyms: brief, passing, short-lived, momentary, ephemeral

56. **foolhardy** (adjective); FOOL-hahr-dee: recklessly bold or daring without thinking about the risks or consequences
synonyms: reckless, rash, imprudent, incautious, impulsive

57. **forbearance** (noun); for-BAIR-uhns: patient self-control, restraint, and tolerance in difficult situations
synonyms: patience, restraint, tolerance, endurance, moderation

58. **foreboding** (noun); for-BOH-ding: fearful apprehension; a feeling that something bad will happen
synonyms: apprehension, anxiety, trepidation, danger, unease

59. **formidable** (adjective); FOR-mid-uh-buhl: eliciting fear or admiration due to remarkable strength, size, intensity, or capability
synonyms: intimidating, commanding, imposing, impressive, fearsome

60. **funereal** (adjective); fyoo-NEER-ee-uhl: having the mournful, solemn, or gloomy character appropriate to a funeral
synonyms: mournful, gloomy, sombre, melancholy, dismal

61. **futility** (noun); fyoo-TIL-i-tee: the quality of being pointless or useless; efforts that achieve no results
synonyms: pointlessness, uselessness, meaningless, failure, ineffectiveness

62. **gargantuan** (adjective); gar-GAN-choo-uhn: enormous in size, extent, or quantity
synonyms: massive, gigantic, colossal, immense, monumental

63. **gingerly** (adverb); JIN-juhr-lee: in a careful and cautious way, often to avoid harm or making a mistake
synonyms: carefully, cautiously, delicately, gently, tentatively

64. **gravity** (noun); GRAV-i-tee: extreme or alarming importance
synonyms: seriousness, solemnity, severity, significance, weightiness

65. **grotesque** (adjective); grow-TESK: comically or repulsively ugly or distorted
synonyms: offensive, deformed, outlandish, unpleasant, ugly

66. **hallowed** (adjective); HAL-ohd: honoured as holy; give respect and importance to something (especially old things)
synonyms: sacred, holy, consecrated, sanctified, venerated

67. **harrowing** (adjective); HAR-oh-ing: being made to feel upset by something that is shocking or frightening
synonyms: distressing, upsetting, traumatic, agonising, painful

68. **hubris** (noun); HYOO-bris: excessive pride or self-confidence in a way that is negative
synonyms: arrogance, conceit, haughtiness, pride, vanity

69. **idyllic** (adjective); eye-DIL-ik: characterised by a serene, joyful, and visually pleasing atmosphere
synonyms: tranquil, picturesque, ideal, peaceful, blissful

70. **immaculate** (adjective); im-MAK-yuh-lit: perfectly clean with no flaws or stains; perfectly neat and tidy
synonyms: spotless, pristine, clean, unblemished, impeccable

71. **imminent** (adjective); IM-uh-nent: likely to happen soon (typically something unpleasant)
synonyms: impending, approaching, near, close, forthcoming

72. **immutable** (adjective); im-MYOO-tuh-bul: fixed and unchangeable, unaffected by the passage of time or external influence

synonyms: unchangeable, fixed, set, rigid, inflexible

73. **imperative** (adjective); im-PER-uh-tiv: of something that is really important and needing immediate attention

synonyms: crucial, critical, vital, necessary, urgent

74. **implacable** (adjective); im-PLAK-uh-bul: unable to be soothed or pacified; holding opinions or feelings that are too strong to be changed

synonyms: unappeasable, unforgiving, relentless, stubborn, unbending

75. **inception** (noun); in-SEP-shun: the starting point of an institution or activity

synonyms: beginning, commencement, start, outset, launch

76. **incessant** (adjective); in-SES-uhnt: continuing without pause or interruption; nonstop

synonyms: unceasing, ceaseless, unending, continual, constant

77. **incognito** (adjective & adverb); in-kog-NEE-toh: having one's true identity hidden

synonyms: disguised, undercover, in disguise, masked, anonymous

78. **ineffable** (adjective); in-EFF-uh-bul: too great or extreme to be described in words

synonyms: indescribable, inexpressible, unimaginable, overwhelming, beyond words

79. **infernal** (adjective); in-FUR-nuhl: relating to hell or the underworld; extremely troublesome or annoying in a way that feels unending or evil

synonyms: hellish, diabolical, accursed, wicked, tormenting

80. **inherent** (adjective); in-HAIR-ent: being an essential and inseparable quality that is naturally a part of something
synonyms: intrinsic, innate, built-in, inborn, natural

81. **inquisitive** (adjective); in-KWIZ-i-tiv: eager to know or learn things; sometimes too curious about other people's affairs

synonyms: curious, probing, nosy, investigative, inquiring

82. **integrity** (noun); in-TEG-ri-tee: a steadfast commitment toward being honest and having strong moral and ethical values

synonyms: honesty, uprightness, probity, rectitude, honour

83. **intercede** (verb); in-ter-SEED: to step in or mediate on behalf of another, often to resolve a dispute or plead for mercy

synonyms: intervene, mediate, arbitrate, negotiate, advocate

84. **intrepid** (adjective); in-TREP-id: fearless; not afraid of anything including danger or challenges

synonyms: fearless, unafraid, undaunted, dauntless, bold

85. **inundate** (verb); IN un dayt: to overwhelm someone with things or people to be dealt with

synonyms: flood, overwhelm, swamp, overload, engulf

86. **invincible** (adjective); in-VIN-suh-buhl: too powerful to be defeated, overcome, or conquered

synonyms: unbeatable, unconquerable, indestructible, unassailable, undefeatable

87. **ire** (noun); EYE-ur: intense anger

synonyms: rage, fury, wrath, indignation, temper

88. **irony** (noun); I-ruh-nee: the expression through language and tone that normally signifies the opposite of what you mean, typically for humorous or emphatic effect
synonyms: sarcasm, cynicism, mockery, satire, dryness

89. **irredeemable** (adjective); ih-ree-DEEM-uh-buhl: incapable of being saved, corrected, or reformed
synonyms: hopeless, unfixable, incurable, lost, beyond repair

90. **irrefutable** (adjective); ih-REF-yuh-tuh-buhl: impossible to deny or prove wrong
synonyms: undeniable, unquestionable, indisputable, conclusive, certain

91. **lament** (verb); luh-MENT: to express sad thoughts and feelings
synonyms: mourn, grieve, sorrow, wail, bemoan

92. **legion** (noun); LEE-jun: a large group of people, especially united by a common purpose
synonyms: multitude, horde, host, crowd, throng

93. **lineage** (noun); LIN-ee-ij: one's direct descent from an ancestor; line of family
synonyms: ancestry, descent, bloodline, family tree, heritage

94. **livid** (adjective); LIV-id: furiously angry
synonyms: furious, angry, incensed, enraged, irate

95. **macabre** (adjective); muh-KAH-bruh: disturbing and strange because of involvement with or depiction of death and injury
synonyms: gruesome, grisly, ghoulish, sombre, morbid

96. **magnanimity** (noun); mag-nuh-NIM-i-tee: being kind and generous especially towards someone you don't like
synonyms: generosity, benevolence, charity, altruism, forgiveness

97. **malevolent** (adjective); muh-LEV-uh-lent: having or showing a wish to cause others harm
synonyms: malicious, wicked, evil-intentioned, spiteful, vindictive

98. **maniacal** (adjective); muh-NAHY-uh-kuhl: exhibiting extremely wild or violent behaviour; showing excessive enthusiasm or obsession

synonyms: frenzied, lunatic, deranged, insane, obsessive

99. **manifest** (verb); MAN-uh-fest: to make something visible, evident, or recognisable through actions or appearance

synonyms: express, display, convey, exhibit, reveal

100. **melancholy** (noun); MEL-un-kol-ee: a deep and long-lasting sadness that is difficult to explain

synonyms: sadness, sorrow, unhappiness, woe, desolation

101. **meticulous** (adjective); muh-TIK-yuh-lus: demonstrating extraordinary precision and careful attention to the finest details

synonyms: thorough, diligent, exacting, conscientious, scrupulous

102. **naiveté** (noun); nah-eev-TAY: a lack of experience, wisdom, or judgement that leads to innocence or gullibility; too trusting of others because of lack of experience

synonyms: innocence, gullibility, simplicity, inexperience, credulousness

103. **nefarious** (adjective); ne-FAR-i-us: wicked or criminal in nature, often associated with immoral or malevolent behaviour or action

synonyms: wicked, evil, sinful, sinister, corrupt

104. **netherworld** (noun); NEH-thur-wurld: a hidden, often sinister place or realm, especially associated with the dead or the underworld

synonyms: underworld, abyss, hell, inferno, afterlife

105. **oblivious** (adjective); ob-LIV-i-us: completely unaware or indifferent to what is happening around oneself

synonyms: unaware, unconscious, heedless, unmindful, inattentive

106. **ominous** (adjective); OM-i-nus: suggesting that something unfavourable or dangerous may occur

synonyms: threatening, menacing, alarming, foreboding, sinister

107. **penance** (noun); PEN-ans: a voluntary act of self-discipline or hardship undertaken to express remorse for past wrongdoings

synonyms: atonement, repentance, self-punishment, amends, reparation

108. **pensive** (adjective); PEN-siv: engaged in, involving, or reflecting deep or serious thought about something that you might be worried about

synonyms: thoughtful, reflective, contemplative, musing, meditative

109. **perennial** (adjective); puh-REN-ee-uhl: existing continuously over a long period or recurring at regular intervals

synonyms: everlasting, unceasing, eternal, timeless, perpetual

110. **peril** (noun); PER-il: serious and immediate danger

synonyms: danger, jeopardy, risk, hazard, insecurity

111. **poignant** (adjective); POYN-yuhnt: deeply affecting one's emotions, often stirring sadness or nostalgia
synonyms: moving, touching, sorrowful, heartfelt, evocative

112. **precarious** (adjective); prih-KAIR-ee-us: not securely held or in position; likely to fall or collapse
synonyms: unstable, dangerous, risky, unsafe, shaky

113. **premonition** (noun); pre-mo-NI-shun: a strong intuitive feeling or warning about an upcoming event, often something bad or unpleasant
synonyms: forewarning, hunch, intuition, warning, omen

114. **prescient** (adjective); PRESH-uhnt: having insight or foresight into future events before they unfold
synonyms: foresighted, prophetic, intuitive, predictive, clairvoyant

115. **pretence** (noun); PREE-tens: pretending with the intention to deceive
synonyms: act, fake, show, façade, mask

116. **preternatural** (adjective); pree-ter-NATCH-er-uhl: beyond what is normal or natural; extraordinary or exceptional in a way that seems supernatural
synonyms: extraordinary, exceptional, supernatural, uncanny, unearthly

117. **primal** (adjective); PRY-muhl: relating to the earliest stages of life or instincts; deep and powerful in a raw or natural way
synonyms: basic, instinctive, ancient, elemental, raw

118. **primordial** (adjective); pry-MOR-dee-uhl: existing from the very beginning of time; ancient and original
synonyms: ancient, earliest, original, primeval, prehistoric

119. **pristine** (adjective); PRIS-teen: in its original condition; fresh and unspoiled

synonyms: unspoiled, untouched, clean, immaculate, perfect

120. **progeny** (noun); PRO-juh-nee: the direct descendants of a person, animal, or plant

synonyms: offspring, children, successors, descendants, heirs

121. **prophecy** (noun); PROFF-uh-see: a prediction or message believed to come from a divine source

synonyms: prediction, forecast, vision, divination, revelation

122. **providence** (noun); PROV-i-dens: the protective care of God or of nature as a spiritual power

synonyms: fate, foresight, divine intervention, guardianship, care

123. **prowess** (noun); PROW-es: exceptional skill, ability, or expertise in a particular field

synonyms: skill, expertise, mastery, capability, proficiency

124. **prudent** (adjective); PROO-dent: exercising careful judgment and foresight when making decisions for the future

synonyms: wise, careful, cautious, sensible, thoughtful

125. **purge** (verb); PURJ: to rid (someone or something) of an unwanted quality, thoughts, or feelings

synonyms: remove, get rid of, eradicate, clear, cleanse

126. **regale** (verb); ri-GAYL: to entertain or amuse someone, often with stories or food

synonyms: entertain, delight, amuse, charm, feast

127. **rekindle** (verb); ree-KIN-dl: to start something again, especially feelings or memories, or to light a fire again

synonyms: revive, renew, reignite, awaken, restore

128. **relinquish** (verb); rih-LING-kwish: to voluntarily give up or let go of something

synonyms: surrender, give up, abandon, forego

129. **remorse** (noun); re-MORS: deep regret or guilt for a wrongfully committed act

synonyms: regret, repentance, guilt, penance, compunction

130. **reprieve** (noun/verb); ri-PREEV: a temporary relief or delay from something unpleasant, or the act of postponing a punishment or negative consequence

synonyms: pardon, respite, suspension, deferment, exemption

131. **reproach** (verb); re-PROACH: to express disapproval or disappointment in somebody's actions; to receive blame or criticism for your actions

synonyms: rebuke, reprimand, scold, admonish, chide

132. **requisite** (adjective); REK-wi-zit: made necessary for any particular purpose

synonyms: necessary, required, obligatory, essential, needed

133. **resilience** (noun); rih-ZIL-yuhns: the ability to recover quickly from difficulties or setbacks

synonyms: toughness, strength, bounce back, recovery

134. **retribution** (noun); re-trib-YOO-shun: punishment or revenge for a serious wrong committed by someone

synonyms: vengeance, revenge, payback, reprisal, recompense

135. **revere** (verb); re-VEER: to hold someone or something in deep admiration and high regard

synonyms: respect, admire, cherish, idolise, honour

136. **ruse** (noun); ROOZ: a trick or strategy intended to deceive

synonyms: trick, ploy, deception, stratagem, hoax

137. **sanctity** (noun); SANK-ti-tee: the state or quality of being holy, sacred, or of ultimate importance

synonyms: holiness, sacredness, purity, divinity, inviolability

138. **scathing** (adjective); SKAY-thing: to be extremely critical of someone and show no respect

synonyms: harsh, severely critical, withering, scorching, piercing

139. **sceptical** (adjective); SKEP-ti-kuhl: having doubts or reservations about the truth or reliability of something

synonyms: doubtful, dubious, unsure, questioning

140. **scruples** (noun); SKROO-puhls: feelings of doubt or hesitation that prevents you from doing something because it is not moral or correct

synonyms: qualms, reservations, misgivings, morality, integrity

141. **searing** (adjective); SEER-ing: extremely intense or powerful, often in reference to pain or emotion

synonyms: blazing, scorching, intense, burning, piercing

142. **sinister** (adjective); SIN-i-ster: giving a sense that something harmful, evil, or threatening is taking place or about to occur

synonyms: menacing, threatening, ominous, malevolent, dark

143. **solace** (noun); SOL-iss: a source of comfort or relief during a time of distress or sorrow

synonyms: comfort, consolation, refuge, support, reassurance

144. **solemn** (adjective); SOL-em: formal and dignified; serious

synonyms: serious, sombre, grave, earnest, dignified

145. **solidarity** (noun); sol-i-DAR-i-ty: unity or fellowship arising toward someone because of common feelings, aims and aspirations

synonyms: unity, unanimity, togetherness, cohesion, alliance

146. **solitude** (noun); SOL-i-tood: the state or situation of being alone

synonyms: aloneness, isolation, seclusion, privacy, solitariness

147. **sombre** (adjective); SOM-buhr: dark or dull in colour or tone; serious and sad

synonyms: gloomy, dark, dull, bleak, melancholy

148. **stealthily** (adverb); STELTH-uh-lee: in a secretive or sneaky manner

synonyms: secretly, covertly, furtively, quietly, slyly

149. **stoic** (adjective); STO-ik: not showing one's feelings even if something bad or painful is happening to you

synonyms: emotionless, indifferent, unfeeling, unmoved

150. **sullen** (adjective); SUHL-en: silently resentful, gloomy, or showing irritation

synonyms: moody, brooding, sulky, glum, morose

151. **sunder** (verb); SUHN-dur: to break or split apart forcibly, especially in a violent or abrupt way

synonyms: sever, split, divide, rend, cleave

152. **supplications** (noun); sup-li-KAY-shuns: humble or earnest requests or prayers, especially to a higher power

synonyms: prayers, pleas, entreaties, petitions, appeals

153. **surpass** (verb); sur-PASS: to go beyond in amount, degree, or excellence

synonyms: exceed, outdo, transcend, excel, outshine

154. **surreal** (adjective); suh-REEL: dreamlike in a strange and bizarre way

synonyms: bizarre, strange, unusual, weird, uncanny

155. **temporal** (adjective); TEM-puh-ruhl: related to time or worldly life, rather than spiritual or eternal matter
synonyms: worldly, earthly, fleeting, time-bound, mortal

156. **thwart** (verb); THWORT: to stop something from happening or someone from succeeding

synonyms: prevent, stop, hinder, obstruct, foil

157. **torment** (noun); TOR-ment: severe physical or mental suffering and pain

synonyms: agony, pain, anguish, suffering, torture

158. **tranquillity** (noun); tran-KWIL-i-tee: a state of peace and calm, where everything is still and quiet

synonyms: calmness, peacefulness, serenity, stillness, quiet

159. **transcendent** (adjective); tran-SEN-dent: beyond or above the range of normal, ordinary, or physical limits; at another level

synonyms: surpassing, exceeding, extraordinary, sublime, divine

160. **trenchant** (adjective); TREN-chuhnt: sharply insightful or penetrating in thought, expression, or style

synonyms: incisive, sharp, keen, acute, forceful

161. **ultimatum** (noun); ul-ti-MAY-tum: a final demand or condition that, if refused, will lead to serious retaliation or conflict

synonyms: final demand, final terms, deadline, warning, claim

162. **unassailable** (adjective); uhn-uh-SAY-luh-bul: impossible to defeat or argue against because of being so strong or certain

synonyms: impregnable, invincible, secure, invulnerable, undeniable

163. **unfathomable** (adjective); un-FATH-uh-muh-bul: impossible or difficult to understand; incomprehensible
synonyms: inscrutable, incomprehensible, indecipherable, enigmatic, mysterious

164. **unsightly** (adjective); un-SYTE-lee: unpleasant to look at; unattractive or ugly in appearance
synonyms: ugly, unattractive, hideous, unpleasant, messy

165. **upended** (verb); up-END-ed: turned upside down or completely reversed
synonyms: overturned, flipped, toppled, disrupted, reversed

166. **valour** (noun); VAL-ur: exceptional bravery and courage, particularly in dangerous or battle situations
synonyms: bravery, courage, heroism, gallantry, fearlessness

167. **vanity** (noun); VAN-i-tee: an excessive focus on or admiration of one's own appearance, abilities, or accomplishments
synonyms: conceit, narcissism, arrogance, self-admiration, self-obsession

168. **vehement** (adjective), VEE-uh-muhnt: showing strong, passionate, or intense feeling, especially in speech or action
synonyms: passionate, forceful, intense, fervent, emphatic

169. **vendetta** (noun); ven-DET-a: a prolonged and bitter quarrel
synonyms: feud, dispute, quarrel, fight, conflict

170. **verdant** (adjective); VUR-dnt: covered in green vegetation; lush and full of life
synonyms: green, leafy, flourishing, rich, grassy

171. **vigilant** (adjective); VIG-i-lant: remaining highly watchful and attentive to potential dangers or challenges
synonyms: watchful, observant, cautious, alert, wary

172. **visage** (noun); VIZ-ij: a person's face, especially when expressing emotion or character
synonyms: face, expression, countenance, appearance, features

173. **vulnerable** (adjective); VUL-ner-a-ble: weak; easily influenced, hurt, or attacked physically and/or emotionally
synonyms: at risk, in danger, unsafe, open to attack, sensitive

174. **waning** (adjective); WAY-ning: gradually decreasing or fading away
synonyms: fading, diminishing, weakening, declining, ebbing

175. **wantonly** (adverb); WON-tuhn-lee: done without regard for right or consequences, often in a cruel or reckless manner
synonyms: recklessly, deliberately, cruelly, maliciously, senselessly

176. **wily** (adjective); WY-ly: skilled at gaining an advantage, especially by using trickery
synonyms: cunning, crafty, sly, scheming, tricky

177. **wrath** (noun); RATH: extreme anger
synonyms: anger, rage, fury, ire, indignation

178. **zealous** (adjective); ZEL-uhs: demonstrating intense passion, energy, and enthusiasm toward a cause or goal
synonyms: passionate, enthusiastic, fervent, devoted, eager

About The Authors

RANJIT RAUNIYAR

RANJIT RAUNIYAR IS AN EDUCATOR, ENTREPRENEUR, AND FORMER investment banker with a lifelong passion for learning and storytelling. He grew up in boarding schools in India - at Dr. Graham's School in the mountains of Kalimpong and The Air Force School in India's capital, New Delhi. He is a graduate of Bowdoin College, The London School of Economics and Wharton, where he was the Editor-in-Chief of *The Wharton Journal.*

Ranjit began his career as an analyst with Goldman Sachs in New York and London, and following his MBA from Wharton, with Credit Suisse in London. He is currently GM for the EMEA region at InstaLILY, a New York-based AI technology startup, and has consulted for IFC (The World Bank) and Bank of America.

Ranjit has a keen interest in writing and has previously written for newspapers and magazines, including *The Wall Street Journal*, *The Tribune*, *Himal Magazine*, etc.

Ranjit lives in Hertfordshire, England, with his wife, Surbhy - a teacher of science and patisserie chef - and their children, Ranveer and Suhani.

SUHANI RAUNIYAR

Suhani is an International Baccalaureate Diploma Programme (IBDP) student at United World College (UWC) Atlantic in Wales, UK, where she is in boarding school alongside students from over 150 countries.

Born in London, she began her education at Devonshire House Prep in Hampstead before moving to India at the age of five, where she attended The British School in New Delhi. She returned to England during the pandemic and resumed her studies at James Allen's Girls' School (JAGS) in Dulwich.

Suhani loves reading, art, debating, swimming, karate, watching movies, spending time with her friends and family, meeting new people, and trying new things. Suhani, with a passion for change and curiosity, is taking an active part in her school life through debate, dance, and student government and is always excited about bringing fresh ideas to life.

With this book, Suhani hopes to share her rich and beautiful cultural heritage - to inspire, educate, and bring this timeless story to a new generation of students and readers, not only at the UWCs, but around the world.

RANVEER RAUNIYAR

RANVEER WAS BORN AND RAISED IN LONDON. HE ATTENDED DEVONSHIRE House Prep in Hampstead before moving to India at the age of five. He spent Grades 3-8 at The British School in New Delhi. He later returned to England to attend Dulwich College.

Ranveer is, at present, a student at UWC Dilijan, in Armenia, studying the IBDP and takes pride in studying with students from 80 countries, each with different goals and aspirations.

Ranveer loves to box, work out, run, swim and play basketball. He enjoys spending time with friends and treasures the moments he shares with his family.

Beyond academics, he is committed to making a difference and is passionate about implementing new ideas and perspectives through school social committees, charitable work, and creative ventures in programming and coding.

With this book, Ranveer is excited to share his rich cultural heritage by bringing this wonderful story of the Ramayana to young readers. He hopes his friends - both current and future - from around the world will enjoy reading this book just as much as he has cherished researching and writing it.

About The Illustrator

SWETHA GIRISHKUMAR

SWETHA GIRISHKUMAR IS A FINE ARTIST FROM KERALA, INDIA, WHO has been passionate about art since childhood.

She earned her degree in Fine Arts from Amity University, Uttar Pradesh (India), and has since applied her creativity across various mediums, including comics, educational games, and books.

Currently based in Hyderabad (India), Swetha is breaking new ground in interactive entertainment as a game artist, crafting captivating visual experiences for casual games. With a deep love for storytelling and design, she continues to explore innovative ways to bring art to life and inspire audiences through her work.

Printed in Dunstable, United Kingdom

80269288R00133